THE TRUTH CHRONICLES

Book VIII: the attack

Tim Chaffey

Illustrated by
Melissa "Inkhana" Mathis

Risen Books
Richmond, Kentucky

2021

The Truth Chronicles (Book 8): The Attack
Copyright © 2021 by Tim Chaffey.
All rights reserved.
www.RisenBooks.com

Risen Books is an imprint of Risen Ministries, LLC

Edited by Reagen Reed

Scripture quotations are taken from the Holy Bible, New King James Version.

This novel is a work of fiction. Characters, plot, and incidents are either products of the author's imagination or used fictitiously. Characters are fictional, and any similarity to people living or dead is purely coincidental, except when used with permission.

ISBN-13: 978-0-9960087-4-7

Printed in the United States of America

For Zoe

PROLOGUE

His heart thumping as if it were about to leap out of his chest, Mr. Li pulled into his driveway like an Indy car driver crossing the finish and slammed the brakes. He leapt from the vehicle and ran toward the front door. A single light shone from the living room of an otherwise dark house.

After fumbling with his keys, he unlocked the deadbolt and doorknob and then entered the house. "Chu? Mei-Lin?" He paused for a moment to listen, but the only sounds he heard were his pulse pounding in his ears and the tinkling windchimes near the garage. He closed the door, took a deep breath, and then hurried to his bedroom. "Chu?"

Finding his room empty, he turned around and hustled to his daughter's room. He opened the door while knocking. "Mei-Lin?" *Where are they?*

His phone buzzed and he immediately yanked it out of his pocket. A wave of dread crashed over him when he saw his wife's name and number on the screen. Ten minutes earlier, an unknown voice had used this same number to threaten his family if he failed to accomplish his appointed task. Despite taking a deep breath to calm himself, his voice shook as he said, "Hello."

"Hi."

He bent nearly double as relief crashed over him. It was Chu. "Where are you? Is everything okay? Is Mei-Lin with you?"

The words came out too fast, but she didn't seem to notice. "Everything is fine. I was just calling to let you know that I will be home soon. Mei-Lin is still in Bits & Bytes, but she texted and said she will leave in a few minutes."

Covering his heart with his free hand, Mr. Li took another calming breath. "Oh, okay. That's great. Drive safely."

"I will. See you soon."

"Okay. I can't wait. I love you, *Xiao baobei.*" His words still spilled out faster than usual. *Did I overdo it with the nickname? No, I often call her that.*

She chuckled. "I love you, too. *Zai jian.*"

"*Zai jian.*"

He hung up the phone, walked into the living room, and slumped down onto the couch. The overwhelming fear for his wife and daughter, followed immediately by the elation of knowing they were safe, caused his body to shake, and he fought to hold back tears. *How can I find out the truth about that time machine? Ask Jax and Izzy to show me? Will that put them in danger too? Sneak into Jax's garage? I'm not even thinking straight now.* He shook his head. *Maybe if I sleep on it.* After standing, he walked to the bathroom and tried to push the troubling thoughts from his mind as he washed up and waited for his family to arrive.

ONE

"Is everyone okay?" Jax asked when the interior light faded to its normal setting.

"What happened?" Izzy scratched the back of his head.

"I'm pretty sure we just time traveled," Micky said.

"But where are we?" JT asked. "And when?"

Jax peered into the darkness. "I'm not sure, but we should be careful." He squeezed the voice-activation button on the steering wheel. "Engage cloak and night vision."

"Cloak engaged," the car's computer voice said as the exterior went nearly pitch black. The whirring of a small motor on the roof barely penetrated the vehicle's interior, which suddenly turned a shade of green as the windows displayed the camera's live video.

"I don't recognize this place," Izzy said.

"It's too dark to even tell." Micky leaned closer to the window.

"Destination confirmed."

"What?" Jax said. "No. Computer, shut down."

The countdown appeared on the windshield. *"Five."*

Jax squeezed the button again. "Cancel destination!"

"Four."

"Turn it off!" Micky said.

"Three."

Lights in the distance caught Jax's eye as he tapped furiously on the windshield display. "I'm trying."

"Two."

That looks familiar. Jax glanced around trying to figure out where they were.

"One."

The car flooded with light again and a second later, the distant illuminations in the passenger window were replaced by something much brighter and closer, although it was still clearly nighttime.

"What's it doing?" JT used the back of Jax's seat to pull herself forward.

"I don't know," Jax said.

"Is it done?" Micky asked.

JT pointed frantically. "Gun!"

Jax glanced out his window and his eyes shot open. Holding a machine gun slung across his chest, a man stood facing them, shielding his eyes. *Pastor Rich's guard!* "Elevate maximum height." The car shot upward so fast he felt like he might be sitting on his own stomach. As soon as they hovered higher than the fence surrounding the compound, Jax clicked the button again. "Head south, full throttle."

"As you wish, Jax." The car lurched forward and soared away from danger. "Is he watching us?"

Izzy and Micky tried to peer out the driver's side window. Still moderately blinded by the flash of light, the guard looked around wildly for the threat, but his gaze remained low. "No, he lost us."

"This is where we rescued Pastor Rich," Jax said. "We gotta get out—"

"Destination confirmed."

"Doesn't look like we have a choice," Izzy said.

"Five."

Micky leaned forward. "But we don't know where it's going!"

"Four."

Jax tapped the option to cancel the request, but the countdown continued.

"Three."

"Cancel destination!"

"Two."

"Come on!" Jax hit the steering wheel.

"One."

JT put a hand on Jax's shoulder. "Hold on."

A brilliant light once again enveloped the car. Jax closed his eyes, but when he opened them a moment later, the brightness remained. *What happened?*

"Where are we now?" Micky asked.

Jax's eyes slowly adjusted. The intense light emanated not from the car's interior, but from bright sunlight and a vast expanse of glittering snow. He squeezed the button. "Descend to ground level." The car responded and slowly crunched into the snow as it came to rest.

"Hey, this looks like the place where the Ark was before it crashed down the mountain." JT twisted to survey the area.

"I think you're right," Izzy said. "But how long will we be here?"

"I don't think we're going to jump again." Jax pointed to the power levels. "Not enough juice."

"What is that?" Micky sniffed the air. "It smells like something's burning."

"I don't smell anything." Jax checked the center console and dash to see if Izzy's spilled drink had shorted out any of the circuits.

"The trunk!" Izzy pointed behind them. "It's coming from back there."

"What?" Jax hit the trunk release button and threw open his door, squinting against the glare.

Wisps of smoke crept from the back of the car as Jax tromped through a knee-deep snowbank. He lifted the trunk and immediately spotted the problem. "No!" A small but steady stream of smoke rose from a custom case built into the left panel. An image of the space-time generator appeared in his mind. *Lord, please don't let it be that.* Jax quickly grabbed two of the nearest bags and flung them into the snow. "Get back here!"

"What's wrong?" Izzy asked as his foot sank deep into the snow. "Oh no!"

Jax yanked a box from the trunk. "Quick, get the fire extinguisher. In that red bag."

Izzy unzipped the bag and pulled out a small extinguisher. "Stand back."

"Wait." Jax tested the temperature of the case by tapping it with his hand several times, letting his hand linger a split second longer each time it touched. *Not too hot.* He unlatched the lid and opened it, allowing smoke to billow upward. "Hit it," he said as he leapt out of the way.

A jet of white powder shot out of the extinguisher as Izzy sprayed the source of the smoke for a few seconds. After setting the canister back in the bag, he and Jax inspected the damage.

JT and Micky ran to the back of the vehicle. "What happened?" Micky asked.

"Is it broken?" As JT leaned closer to the trunk, she covered her mouth and coughed.

"Not sure yet." Jax waved his hand rapidly over the combination of smoke and powder that wafted above the case. "Pray that it isn't the STG or we'll be stuck here."

"What do you mean 'stuck'?" Micky asked.

Jax clenched his teeth, trying to calm his rising frustration. "I mean, there's no way we'll ever get home." His voice came out angrier than he had intended.

"What?" Micky clutched at his sleeve. "No!"

Jax twisted his shoulder to pull his shirt away from her. "The space-time generator is what makes time travel possible." *Stay calm and focus.* He closed his eyes for a second, trying to block the fear invading his mind. "Let's all try to relax. We don't even know if it's damaged."

Izzy bent over and put his hands on his knees. "It'd better not be."

"What do we do if it's broken?" Her voice edged with panic, Micky leaned over the trunk. "We have to get home."

Jax let out a frustrated sigh. "Micky, please."

"What? How can you expect me to be calm?"

JT put a hand on her shoulder. "Micky."

"Because we don't know if we're stuck yet, so there's no point in freaking out right now." He turned back to the trunk and blew into the container to clear some of the air. The fumes dispersed for a brief moment, and his heart sank at the glimpse of melted sheaths and blackened wires. *Where is it?* A knot formed in his gut as he bent lower and continued to blow softly to see into the cabinet. Tucked further forward in the case, the space-time generator sat a couple of inches away from the damaged materials and appeared to be unscathed.

Jax breathed a deep sigh of relief and stepped away from the car, but his legs wobbled like jelly and he collapsed in the snow.

"I knew it. We're stranded." Micky locked her fingers behind her head and looked up at the sky.

"Jax? Jax?" JT asked, bending over him. "How bad is it?"

Jax stared up at her as the overpowering sense of relief gave way to rational thought. "I think the STG survived."

Izzy slowly lifted his head. "Seriously?"

"I think so." Jax nodded. "But the wires look pretty bad."

"Let me see." Izzy moved closer to the vehicle and stared carefully into the trunk while waving his hand over the cabinet. He whistled and shook his head. "Yeah, they're a mess. Did your dad pack any spare wire?"

"I don't think so." Jax shivered as the cold wetness of snow seeped through the back of his pants. He stood and brushed himself off. Leaning over the trunk, he stared at the thin, flexible threads again. "It's definitely not good."

Micky dug through her bag, which Jax had tossed in the snow. She pulled out a sweatshirt and slipped it on. "It's freezing out here. Can we talk about it in the car?"

"Go ahead. I've got to check a few more things first," Jax said.

"Come on, girl," Micky said.

After JT found a sweatshirt in her bag and put

it on, she joined Micky in the car.

Jax traced the wires toward the top-secret power supply his father had invented. "I think the Cube should be fine."

"What about the charging panels?" Izzy asked.

Jax lifted his head and inspected the seemingly unharmed black case on the other side of the trunk. "Over there. But let me check the wiring." He ran a finger along a line from the center of the trunk lid to a wire harness next to the nearest hinge, and then down to the compartment that housed the Cube. "Looks good. Let's put them out."

"Micky's right. It is freezing out here." Izzy blew warm air on his hands and then rubbed them together. "Where are the panels?"

"That black case." Jax pointed to the other side of the trunk.

Izzy grabbed the case but then paused. "Do you think charging the batteries will let the computer take over again?"

"Not with that mess. We don't know how bad it is yet, but I don't think we'll be time traveling anywhere until we sort all that out." Jax glanced at the fused wires, then turned to stare down the mountain slope. "We should head toward that abandoned village down the mountain. We'll need to figure out how we're going to repair this, and I'm pretty sure we won't be able to fix the wiring if our hands are numb."

"Abandoned?" Izzy grinned. "I think you're forgetting that it had at least three inhabitants."

Jax scratched his head as the images of two velociraptors and a carnotaurus flashed into his mind. "Oh, I remember. Do you think they'll still be there?"

Izzy shrugged. "We've already had enough go wrong." He scanned their surroundings. "No need to add to it."

Jax scooped up two of the bags from the snow and packed them in the trunk. "Well, we don't need to go into the village. I just want to get off this mountain. It'll be easier to work if the weather is warmer."

"I agree." Izzy picked up a bag and handed it to Jax.

"You have the panels?"

Izzy nodded.

Jax returned the final item to its place, made sure nothing was smoldering anymore, and then closed the lid.

Izzy unlatched the case and opened up the dual solar panels like a book before snapping them into place on the center of the trunk.

"Let's go make sure everything else is still working." Jax walked to the driver's door and climbed in. He started the car and checked the gauges, noticing that the charging light blinked green. *Good.* Cranking the heater to High, he caught JT's gaze in the rearview mirror.

"What's the plan?" JT asked.

After closing his door, Izzy faced the girls. "We need to do some repairs, but we want to get off this mountain first."

"That sounds good."

"How long will that take?" Micky asked.

"To get to the village? Probably a little over an hour, if I remember correctly. Repair the car? I have no idea." Jax instructed the car to rise a couple of feet and then steered it toward the slope that led to the abandoned village. He glanced at his watch. "It's already 11:30 at night back home."

JT yawned. "11:30? No wonder I'm so tired."

Jax glanced at her in the rearview mirror. "Well, assuming San Dimas Time, if we can get this working in the next eight hours, we can just register at the camp in the morning and no one will know we were gone."

"And what if we can't get it working?" Izzy asked.

Jax bit his lip and shrugged. "I don't know."

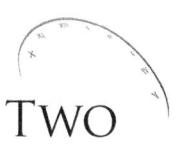

TWO

Jax yawned and stretched his arms and legs within the confines of the driver's seat. Trying to remain alert, he lightly slapped his cheek before leaning his head forward into the cool air streaming from the vent. The bright sunlight ahead made it even more difficult to keep his eyes open. Izzy snored quietly with his head resting against the passenger window. JT and Micky were curled up in the back. Like Izzy, they had been sleeping for much of the last hour.

According to the car's thermometer, the temperature had risen during their descent down the mountain, from 22 degrees to 56 degrees Fahrenheit. Deep snow now yielded to gray rock, brown dirt, and yellowed grass interspersed with patches of murky slush.

Jax rubbed his eyes. *Why did the car pick those three places? The Ark site? Pastor Rich's rescue? And where was that other one?* He had clearly seen two sets of lights in the distance. *Where was that? Why did it look so familiar? It must've been a place I've traveled to.* He bent forward and allowed the cool air to strike his face. *No, not where I've traveled to, but where I've traveled from. That's it. Other than the garage, those were the last three places the time machine departed from.*

The car rounded a corner and the abandoned village lay before them. Jax engaged the outside microphone and listened for any hints of danger. *It looks the same.* He shook his head. *Of course, it was yesterday. So weird.* While it had been a year since they explored the village, in this time it was only one day.

With the cloak engaged, he hovered around the town for a couple of minutes. Satisfied that the velociraptors and carnotaurus had moved on, Jax directed the vehicle toward the middle of the open field adjacent to the large shed. With a slight bump, the time machine came to a rest on the ground.

JT stirred and caught Jax's attention in the rearview mirror. "Why did we stop?"

"We're at the village."

"Already?" JT rubbed her eyes before bolting upright. "Did you—"

"Don't worry. I didn't see any sign of those dinosaurs." Jax shook Izzy's shoulder. "Wake up."

Izzy groaned and shifted in his seat.

After checking their surroundings again, Jax popped the trunk. "Come on, Iz. Time to fix this thing."

"Can I help?" JT asked.

"Of course." Jax climbed out of the car and tilted his seatback forward.

JT grabbed the hand Jax offered and pulled

herself out of the back. "Thanks." She breathed in deeply. "It's a lot warmer here."

"Definitely." Jax lifted the trunk lid. "I'm not sure if there will be room for three of us to work in this space, but at the very least, you can be on the lookout."

"I can do that." JT helped him unload the bags from his side of the trunk. "What do we do if a predator shows up?"

"I guess that depends on how big it is and how quickly we need to elevate to safety." Jax inclined his head toward the bags on the ground. "It should only take about ten seconds to toss these back in, so just try to give us a bit of warning."

"Okay."

Jax ducked into the trunk and opened the STG compartment. Thankfully, the smoke was no longer an issue, giving him a clear view of the damage. "What a mess." He tried to separate a couple of the wires, but the outer sheaths had melted together. "That's not good."

"What's not good?" JT asked.

He stood and faced her. "Looks like a couple of wires are fried. We'll probably need to pull some from a different part of the car to replace them."

"That doesn't sound too hard."

"No, but my dad won't be happy."

She smiled. "I'm sure he'll just be glad if you make it back in one piece."

Izzy opened his door and staggered out. "I'm too tired for this. You realize that even though it's afternoon here, it's really the middle of the night for us, right?"

"Yes, and I also know that I'm the only one who hasn't had any sleep." His own exhaustion weighing on him, Jax battled the urge to lash out. "Let's figure out what needs to be done, and if we need to find a safe spot to sleep, we can do that afterward, okay?"

"Yeah." Izzy yawned. "Sorry, I didn't mean to sound grumpy. How does it look?"

Jax stepped aside to give Izzy a clear view of the jumbled mass. "We could probably pull a wire from one of the rear speakers and cut the lengths we need from it."

Izzy nodded. "Yeah, that should work."

"There's a little toolbox up there." Jax pointed toward the front of the trunk.

Micky appeared at JT's side. "Looks like the guys don't want our help."

"They just don't want us to fix it faster than they can." JT laughed. "Actually, you can help me keep watch. This is where we escaped from some pretty vicious dinosaurs." While Jax crawled halfway into the trunk and peered at the rear speaker connection, JT recounted their close call in the village.

Jax pushed himself back to his feet. "We'll

probably need to pull off some trim to get enough wire."

"What about the silver cable?" Izzy asked. "Does it have one?"

"I forgot all about that." He held his breath. *God, please don't let it be damaged.* Pushing aside the charred copper wires, Jax spotted the silver rod covered in extinguisher powder. He and his dad had fashioned it to power the STG. As he brushed off the white residue, his stomach tightened. The plastic sheath had melted away and the thick wire, now blackened in the same spot, had sagged and cracked. "Oh no." He stepped back and shook his head at Izzy.

Izzy bent down to examine it. After a few seconds, he placed his elbow on the car's rear fender panel and buried his head in the crook of his arm. "What are we gonna do?"

"What's so special about that one?" JT asked.

Jax took a steadying breath. "It's the one that carries all the juice to the STG, and it's in bad shape."

JT's face turned white, and Micky's eyes grew wide.

"We have to repair it," Izzy shook his head slowly as he rubbed his temple. "It looks like it overheated, which is what started the fire. It probably cracked when we put out the fire in the cold air. It cooled too rapidly, and without the sheathing to hold it in place, it fractured."

"So how are we going to fix it?" Micky finished pulling her green hair back into its ponytail. "Isn't the melting temperature of silver nearly 1000 degrees Celsius?"

Izzy stared off in the distance. "Yeah, 961.68 degrees, to be precise or 1,763.2 degrees Fahrenheit." His voice trailed off, as if he were thinking out loud rather than showing off.

"Let me guess, you guys used silver because you needed the highest possible conductivity, right?" JT asked.

Jax nodded.

"So couldn't we just repurpose more of the copper from the car?" Micky asked. "Its conductivity is almost as high."

Jax shrugged. "But a copper wire would have to be thicker, and then it wouldn't fit into the STG opening."

"Plus, we don't have a mold for it," Izzy said.

"Couldn't we make one?" Micky looked at Izzy and tilted her head slightly.

Izzy held his arms out. "From what?"

Micky glanced back toward the mountain slope. "From rock."

"We don't have the tools. And, besides, how could we ever make it just the right size with what we can find here?"

An idea leapt into Jax's mind and he nudged

Izzy out of the way to study the cable again. "Actually, I think Micky's got a point." He stood and faced his three friends. "We could use the undamaged part of the cable to make a mold from some sandstone. It would take a while, but it might work."

Izzy rubbed his chin and raised an eyebrow. "Even if we could use copper, which we probably can't, how in the world would we melt it? We'd need to get the fire up to 1,085 degrees Cel—" He spun and reached for the tool kit in the trunk. "Does your dad keep a propane torch in here?"

Jax's heart leapt and then sank just as quickly. The small box was unlikely to contain such a tool.

Seconds later, Izzy slammed the case shut and groaned. "Well, we have screwdrivers, drill bits, a small hammer, and some wrenches." He clenched his jaw and strode several steps away. Snatching up a palm-sized rock, he yelled and threw it as far as he could. "Why?"

Micky hurried to Izzy while JT caught Jax's eye, her face etched with concern.

How are we ever going to make it back home? Jax took a deep breath. While he wanted to shout his frustration too, he needed to appear confident and positive. As he followed JT toward Izzy, he leaned close and whispered, "Don't forget to keep a lookout."

"Oh yeah. I forgot."

While JT broke off to scan the area, Micky put a hand on Izzy's shoulder. "It's okay."

Izzy spun and faced them, his eyes moist with tears. "No, it's not." He looked at the ground and shook his head. "This is all my fault."

"What are you talking about?" JT said.

He held his arms out and looked around. "This. Us being stuck here. All of it. It's my fault."

"How can you say that?" Micky asked.

"It was my drink that spilled and shorted things out. If I wasn't such a klutz, none of this would've happened."

Jax remained silent. The very same thoughts had occurred to him while he piloted the vehicle down the mountain. But escalating the situation would not help matters.

"I'm so sorry." Izzy dropped to the ground. "Because of me, we're never going to get home. We'll never see our family or friends again."

"Don't say that," Micky said.

"Why not?" Izzy punched the ground. "It's true."

"You don't know that."

"And you don't know how we can ever fix it." Izzy glared up at her. "None of us do."

Micky bit her lip and caught Jax's eye before tilting her head toward Izzy, as if pleading with Jax to jump in.

Jax took a deep breath. "Okay, that's enough.

Assigning blame isn't going to do us any good, and neither is whining about it." He matched Izzy's glare until Izzy dropped his gaze. "We'll figure out a way to get home."

Izzy traced a line in the dirt. "How? I doubt the people of this time have figured out how to work with silver yet. It could take us months or maybe even years to get the right tools and materials to remake that wire. How will we survive until then?"

"We'll figure it out. They had metalworking before the Flood," JT said. "Well, at least they had bronze and iron."

"Yeah, but after the Flood, they had to start over again." Izzy looked up at them. "And according to our history books, silversmithing wasn't developed until several thousand years before our time, which would be centuries from now."

JT glanced at him but then resumed searching the tree line to their left. "But I'll bet the people at Babel had better technology than their immediate descendants. Like the Flood, the Babel event created a technological reset. There might have been a couple of groups who took the knowledge of metalworking with them once they scattered, but most of the cultures probably would've needed to start over."

Izzy sighed and the fight seemed to be leaving him. "Okay, let's assume that's true. How would that help us now? We still have to find or make a forge and find more silver somewhere. And we have to eat in the meantime."

"At least we know what we need to do. I don't know how much that helps us," Jax said. "But I do know that I've got the three smartest friends in the world and we'll figure it out." He glanced at Micky and winked. "Well, two smartest friends. Besides"—Jax lightly kicked Izzy's shoe—"if we are stuck here, at least I'm stuck with you guys."

Izzy shook his head and fought back a smile. "Thanks."

Jax helped Izzy to his feet. "If any of us are going to figure out how to get home, it's going to be the genius valedictorian."

Izzy laughed and wiped his eyes with the back of his hand. "You had to remind me, didn't you?"

"Yeah, no pressure," JT said sarcastically. "Seriously, though, if anyone is going to get us out of this, it's God. We should pray."

Jax smiled. "Best idea I've heard all day."

Three

"I'm still not sure this is a good idea," JT said as she climbed into the back seat.

Micky plopped down next to her. "It seems safe to me."

"That's because you didn't see the dinosaurs that chased the guys."

Here we go again. Izzy sat down and closed the passenger door. "It should be fine as long as someone keeps watch from above. We'll just quickly search all the buildings for any signs of metalworking."

Jax plugged his phone into the charging port, started the vehicle, and then directed it to hover at ten feet and head into the village.

"Why are you charging your phone?" Micky asked. "It's not like it'll work here."

"No, but I think we should all have our phones fully charged. We can use our translators as basic transmitters." Jax held up a pair of the earbuds from the science fair. "The phones have a range of about a quarter mile without cell towers, so if we get separated for any reason, we can still communicate."

"Don't we need one of those devices you had in your shirt?" Micky pointed toward his collar.

Jax shook his head. "No, because we all speak

the same language. The collar piece is just a speaker that projects the translation of my speech in whatever language is selected on the app. The earbuds by themselves will work as transmitters."

"Ah, I wondered about that," JT said.

"That's a good idea." As Izzy stared at the ground several feet beneath his window, an image of the damaged silver cable appeared in his mind. He let out a frustrated sigh. "Even if we find some sort of smelting furnace or forge, we'll still need some extra silver."

"Why?" Micky asked.

Izzy turned a little in his seat to look at her. "Well, if we carve a mold into rock, some of the liquid metal will leak into the porous areas."

"Well, let's worry about that later. Oh, you said there were drill bits in the trunk. If there's a three-eighths bit, then that will be the perfect diameter to make the mold." Jax pointed to the storehouse to the right. Its main door had been torn from the wooden hinges and the frame around it had been ripped to shreds by the carnotaurus. "We've already checked out that building and the main hall directly ahead. So where would you like to start?"

"I say we search the main hall again," Izzy said. "There was an altar in there, but we didn't really get a chance to explore it because of those raptors. Plus, it's not like we were actually looking for anything specific before."

As Jax maneuvered the vehicle toward the front door of the main hall, Izzy spotted a familiar sight. "The note!"

"Yeah, what about it?" Jax asked.

Izzy's eyes widened as he pointed. "It's *nailed* to the door."

"So they did use metal," Micky leaned closer to the window to get a better look.

"But what kind is it?" JT asked.

"Only one way to find out." Jax lowered the car to a few inches above the ground.

"Even if it's something that's useful for us, we can't pull the nails from the door," JT said.

"Why not?" Jax held his arm out. "This place is completely abandoned."

"Because we're trying not to change the past." Izzy opened his car door. "Remember what we thought the note said? It sounded like a message for a couple of people who might come back through here."

JT leaned between the two front seats. "And if they do, they'll need to find that note, or else they may not meet up with the rest of their group. And that could drastically change things."

"Well, let's check it out before we make any decisions. If they're silver, we may need them." Jax opened his door and paused. "I think us being stuck here would also change things considerably."

After climbing out, he hurried to inspect the nail, and Izzy followed close behind. "I don't think it's iron—no oxidation—and I doubt they were making steel." Jax studied the lower nail. "It doesn't look like aluminum, either. What do you think?"

Izzy touched the silver-gray metal. "I agree. Probably not aluminum. I suppose it could be silver, but I think it's probably tin."

Jax grimaced. "Let's hope not."

Izzy rubbed the back of his neck and struggled to put his thoughts into words. Tin had such a low melting point compared to the other metals they had discussed. If it were tin, they were no nearer knowing whether the people of this time had the capability of working with silver.

Jax pointed to the lower nail. "We should take this one just in case."

Izzy pushed open the door. "Let's just poke around a little bit first."

Jax spun back toward the car. "If you two are staying out here, you should hover above the building and keep watch."

"Okay." JT climbed out of the back seat and jumped into the driver's spot. Within a few seconds, the car rose from the ground. The window slid down and she said, "We'll just be right out here."

"Sounds good." Jax gave her a thumbs up. "Oh, and turn on the cloak, too."

She nodded.

"After you," Izzy said as he held the door open for Jax.

The great hall looked exactly as Izzy remembered it. The altar rested between the two massive wooden tables and beyond them, built into the back wall, was the huge stone fireplace. "I'll go around this side." Izzy pointed to their right.

"Then I guess I'll go this way." Jax headed toward the left wall.

Quickly moving around the room, they searched for further evidence of metalworking. A minute later, they met near the fireplace.

"Look at these stones." Izzy leaned down and ran his hand along some scratches in the base of the fireplace.

"Well, I'm not sure what made those." Jax leaned in for a closer inspection. "Maybe some sort of metal instrument like a poker."

"That's what I was thinking." Izzy looked down into the fireplace for a moment before facing Jax. "I didn't see anything else."

"Neither did I. Let's check out that altar again, and then we'll search the rest of the town."

The altar displayed similar scrapes in the rock, but nothing else caught the boys' interest. They walked back to the front door and as they stepped through, the car appeared in front of them. JT excitedly waved them over.

Izzy instinctively checked both directions. *Oh no, not another dinosaur.*

"Is everything okay?" Jax asked.

"Yeah, it's fine, but we think we may have found what we're looking for." JT pointed ahead. "Just past that building at the end of the road. You can walk if you'd like. The coast is clear."

Izzy took a deep breath and tried to slow his heartrate. He stared in the direction she indicated. *Road* was a generous word for the trail in front of them. They had not been to that side of the town before. "What's over there?"

"We're not completely sure, but if it's what we think it is, then we might be in luck." JT tilted her head forward. "Come on."

Jax jogged ahead and Izzy fell into step behind him. They passed two small houses on either side of the narrow path. As he moved beyond the second home on the left, Jax slowed to a halt and stared at a stone structure on the ground.

"Is it a stone oven?" JT asked as she lowered the vehicle alongside him.

Izzy approached it slowly. "It may have been, but it's just a pile of rubble now."

While Micky hopped out of the car and circled the front end, Jax bent down and studied the collection of stones and plaster that stood a little lower than his knees. "Hey, check this out." He pointed to a lump of material on the ground next to the oven. "I think this might be a pile of slag."

Izzy looked over Jax's shoulder at the blackened mass of stone and metal. "Looks like it." His lips turned up slightly. "Maybe these people actually are capable of working with silver."

"I guess we'll be heading home after all," Micky bounced on her toes and clapped her hands.

"Not so fast." Izzy pointed at the ruined oven. "There's no way we can use this one."

"Can we build our own?" JT asked.

"I think so," Jax said. "But we don't have enough metal yet, and we wouldn't have any fuel to get the fire hot enough. We could make our own charcoal, but that would take—"

A roar from the other side of the village filled the air, causing all four teens to jump. As they stared at each other with eyes wide open, the unmistakable pounding of footsteps sent tremors up through their feet like tiny earthquakes.

JT screamed before jumping out of the car and climbing into the back seat.

"Quick. We have to go. Like now." Jax bolted toward the car and dropped into the driver's seat.

Izzy followed Micky to the passenger side. While she ducked in, he glanced down the road toward the main hall and his fears were confirmed. The carnotaurus stepped past a building and turned in their direction. Still a safe distance away, it roared and lumbered toward them. "Go!"

"Get in!" Wide eyed, Jax stared at the rearview mirror. "Elevate twenty feet and engage cloak."

The car rose out of danger, and a flicker on the windows indicated they were now viewing the outside world through the multi-camera's feed.

"Let's get out of here," JT said as she stared out of the tiny triangular window near Jax's headrest.

Jax guided the car back over the village while the carnotaurus sniffed the air and searched for its prey.

"Is that what chased you last time?" Micky asked.

"I think so," Izzy said. "If it wasn't that one, it was one just like it."

Micky shook her head slowly while facing the rear window. "That thing is awesome."

"Try being five feet away from its mouth."

"No thanks," Micky said. "That was close enough."

"What do we do now?" JT asked. "It's pretty obvious that it's not safe here."

Izzy glanced at Jax and the turned toward the girls. "First, we need to look for a piece of rock that can serve as our mold. The sooner we have that, the sooner we can bore a hole in it."

Jax nodded. "Right. And then I think we should head back to where we saw that caravan last time."

"Why?" Micky asked.

JT leaned forward. "Oh yeah! They were shooting arrows at that T-rex. Of course"—she thrust her chin out thoughtfully—"they might have been tipped with bone or stone, but …"

"Exactly. If their arrows were tipped with metal, we might be able to use them." Jax turned the car toward a bend that angled down away from the village and the mountain.

"And if we can't?" Izzy asked.

Jax held his palms up. "Then we find out where the people went and see if there's any way for us to get some silver."

Micky sighed and her shoulders dropped. "It's not like they're going to trade with us, and we don't have anything to give them anyway. 'Hey, ancient people, would you like my new cell phone?'"

JT giggled, but then her brow furrowed. "Wait, are you talking about stealing what we need?"

Jax shook his head. "I don't know. We might have to, although that's not what I'd prefer. We should be praying about it. And if we find some, I'm pretty sure we could make our own mudbrick oven to melt it."

JT rubbed her hands together. "Well, let's hit the road then."

Jax caught Izzy's eye. "Road? Where we're going, we don't need roads."

Izzy spoke the last phrase at the same time and laughed.

FOUR

JT stared at the lightly worn trail they had been following for the past hour. With the car cloaked and hovering eight feet above the ground, the ride had been rather uneventful, and JT kept herself alert by focusing on how they could fix the silver cable ... and trying to ignore her complaining stomach.

Jax snored softly in the passenger seat while Izzy and Micky slept in the back. JT closed her eyes. *Lord, thank You for protecting us during those jumps through time and in the village. Please continue to watch over us and help us to find what we need to get home. And please help Izzy get through whatever has been bugging him lately.*

As she watched the rather barren landscape slowly drift by, she considered that part of her prayer had already been answered. After escaping the village, they had spotted a seam of sandstone a couple of feet thick near the base of the mountain. The roots of a tree had knocked loose a few chunks of the relatively soft stone, allowing Izzy to find a football-size piece. *Thank You, God.* JT smiled. *Please let that work well enough for a mold.*

A patch of trees in the distance caught her attention. As it drew closer, she estimated that it covered several acres. A small sparkling river wound into the grove and reappeared on the opposite side. *I wonder if that's the oasis Jax mentioned.* She glanced at her sleeping friends and her stomach grumbled. *Shouldn't be any harm in checking it out. Maybe we'll find some fruit.*

The daylight had allowed the Cube to keep half its charge while they hovered. But now, with the sun descending lower in the sky, the power supply would also be dropping soon. After double-checking her surroundings and making a mental note of precisely where the trail lay in relation to the trees, she veered left.

When they were a few hundred yards away from the trees, JT gently shook Jax's shoulder. "Jax."

He mumbled something and then shifted away from her, still sound asleep.

She shook him a little harder. "Hey, wake up."

He jolted and took in a quick breath. His eyes shot open and he turned to face her, his spiked hair completely disheveled. "What's wrong?"

"Nothing." She tilted her head toward the windshield. "Is this the oasis you told me about?"

He stared at the window and yawned. "Could be. Where's the trail?"

JT pointed to his window. "Just back there a little bit. I thought we might be able to find some food and water here."

He rubbed his eyes and spoke through another

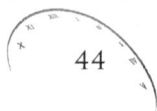

yawn. "Sounds good."

"I'll circle it one time first to make sure it's safe," JT said. "I am not interested in seeing any more of the local wildlife."

Jax nodded. "How long was I asleep?"

"About an hour. Did it help?"

"Doesn't feel like it yet." He checked his watch. "It's after 3:00 A.M. back home. No wonder I'm tired."

"Me too." JT tipped her head toward the back. "Should we wake them up?"

"I'd prefer to just talk with you." Jax grinned at her.

She blushed a little and returned the smile.

"But I suppose they should be awake for this."

While Jax woke Izzy and Micky, JT guided the car around the oasis. A few dozen palm trees lined what looked like a pond but was actually a wide section of the river. Trees bearing green fruit and a few with red fruit grew a short distance from the water. With no sign of any large predators, a variety of birds and some antelope-like mammals were taking advantage of this small retreat.

She brought the car to a halt within reach of a large tree flaunting green fruit. "They look sort of like pears. Do you think they're edible?"

"I sure hope so. We definitely need something to eat," Izzy said.

"Give me one." Jax held out his hand. "I'll try it."

She lowered the window, plucked one of the fist-sized fruits, and handed it to Jax.

He slowly turned it over in his hand and then smelled it. After wiping it on his shirt, he took a small bite. "It does taste a bit like a pear. It's weird, though. It's juicy, but not as sweet. Grab some more."

JT grabbed about a dozen more, handing each one to Jax before reaching for the next. "Is that enough?"

"Maybe." Izzy pointed ahead. "Let's get some of those red ones too."

A choked gurgle jerked JT's attention back to Jax, who reached for his throat and gasped for air as he stared wild-eyed at the fruit in his hand.

Instantly, JT's hand went to his shoulder. "Jax?" Her insides twisted into a knot and her heart raced. "What's wrong?"

Jax broke into a smile and laughed. "Gotcha."

After catching her breath, JT punched his shoulder. "Don't ever do that again." She punched him again.

He caught her fist in his hand and squeezed it, grinning as Izzy kicked his seat from behind.

"Yeah, not funny, man," Izzy said.

"Yeah." Micky giggled. "You got my hopes up for a minute."

"Sorry." Releasing JT's hand, Jax looked down and ran his fingers through his hair. "Come on, though. We haven't had any fun since we got here. I thought it might be good to have a laugh."

JT narrowed her eyes at him as her pulse relaxed. "I could use a laugh, but that wasn't funny."

"Okay, I nominate Jax to test those red ones," Micky said.

Jax shrugged. "No problem." He looked at JT. "And I promise I won't fake being poisoned."

"You'd better not." JT moved the car to another tree and plucked at least twenty plum-sized fruit before Jax insisted they had enough.

"Do you think it's safe to drink the water?" Micky asked. "I finished my water from home, and I'm getting pretty thirsty."

Jax turned and faced her. "I'm sure it isn't the most pristine water in the world. I mean, it comes from the mountains, which is good, but it probably has some animal waste in it."

Micky rolled her eyes as JT watched in the rearview mirror. "That's a lovely thought."

"I've got my hiking backpack with a three-liter bag in it," JT said. "It has a filter."

"We can all refill our water bottles." Jax picked up Izzy's empty soda cup from the floor. "And we've got this. There might be some other containers in the trunk too."

JT guided the vehicle along the river away from the trees.

"Where are you going?" Jax asked.

"To get some water. I just didn't want to set down in the middle of the trees where a predator could be hiding. Out in the open, we'll be able to see anything coming."

"Good idea." Jax winked at her. "Izzy and I don't usually think about things like that."

"And that's why you bring me along on these trips. Also probably why you've encountered more things with sharp teeth than your average elasmobranchologist."

Carefully checking their surroundings, JT lowered the vehicle near the bank of the river. She popped the trunk and climbed out. After emptying some of the items from her backpack to make room for a full water bladder, she attached the filter to the opening.

Jax reached for the container. "I'll fill it up."

"Oh, thanks." JT pointed to a small valve on the filter. "Just open that and hold the whole thing under the water. It should fill right up."

"Cool." Jax stepped to the river's edge and then plunged the bag into the glimmering water. "Is there an easy way to use some of this filtered stuff to put in my bottle?"

JT rubbed her upper arms to warm up. "Yeah, just disconnect the filter and pour it."

Jax followed her instructions and then topped off the bladder.

"I'm glad you have that filter," Micky said. "Who knows what kind of pathogens are lurking in that water."

"Me too," JT said. "I always keep it in that backpack. I thought it might come in handy if we went hiking at camp. I never imagined this scenario though."

Jax stood and raised an eyebrow. "Hey, there's still a chance that we can make it to camp in time." He handed her the full bag and she slid it into place in her backpack.

"You really are an optimist. I wish I was as confident as—" Izzy's eyes grew wide as he stared at the river.

JT turned as a large bird rocketed past them and glided about a foot above the water. *That's not a bird. It looks like a ... like a flying reptile.* The animal opened its long mouth, allowing its lower jaw to skim into the river. A second later, it snapped its jaw shut with a fish wriggling in its beak.

"Awesome!" Jax and Izzy said in unison.

"Is that a pterodactyl?" JT asked.

Jax stared at the winged creature as it rose in the air to their left. "I think it's a pteranodon. Notice the large crest on the back of its head? Pterodactyls don't have those."

A high-pitched squawk rang out to their right. As JT pivoted to search the sky, the afternoon sun blinded her. She blinked repeatedly and shielded her eyes with her hand. Bit by bit, five more figures took shape, each one seemingly larger than the next. Then without warning, the pteranodons dove toward the teens. "Get in the car!" JT took two steps and then screamed, dropping to the ground. One of the creatures zipped overhead, its claws missing her by inches. As she sprang to her feet and climbed into the back seat, another pteranodon landed about twenty feet away. The flying beast used its wings as forelimbs to shamble toward them. The top of its head must have been over ten feet in the air.

Jax climbed in and shut the door. "Are you okay?"

"Yes," JT said as she tried to catch her breath.

Micky piled in next to her, and a moment later Izzy scrambled into the passenger seat and slammed the door. Only a few feet away from the front of the vehicle, the pteranodon continued its awkward walk. JT craned her neck to look out the back window. Three of the creatures had soared upward and were banking in the air as if readying for another pass. The last one had landed behind them and lumbered clumsily in their direction. "Go!"

As Jax directed the car up, the pteranodon nearest them stood on two legs to rear back and strike the hood, but they moved just in time.

While Jax continued their ascent, he let out a low whistle.

"Hurry! The other ones are coming right at us." JT stared wide-eyed out the back window.

"Engage cloak," Jax said. After the windows flickered, he turned the car back in the direction of the river.

"Why are you going back there?" JT's words came out louder than she had intended.

"Because they saw us moving in the other direction," Jax said. "And now that they can't see us anymore, we should be able to lose them this way."

Jax was right. A minute later, the teens were safely drifting back toward the trail. The six large pteranodons had given up their pursuit and now squawked at each other on the riverbank.

JT sighed and allowed her head to roll against the side of the car. *Lord, thank You for sparing us once again.* Her stomach grumbled, so she grabbed one of the red fruits off the pile and took a bite. Its flavor and juiciness reminded her of a plum, but its texture was more like a peach. She held up another one and offered it to Micky, who happily accepted it.

Soon the car was silent other than the sounds of four teens chomping on their crispy and juicy meal. After finishing her fruit and setting its core on the floorboard, JT pulled out her sweatshirt and stretched it across her legs. "Can we try to avoid any more close encounters, please?"

Jax chuckled. "Why? We can't have a time travel adventure without being attacked and nearly killed by creatures that most people have never even seen. Besides, you gotta admit those pteranodons were really cool."

Izzy cleared his throat. "Hey, I've got a question about the Bible."

"Whoa, transition much?" Micky pretended to grab her neck. "I think I just got whiplash."

JT slapped her shoulder playfully. She certainly had no objection to talking about something other than what creature might attack them next, or how they might get home, or how they might ruin the future through their actions here. "Don't listen to her, Iz. Go ahead."

"First, I'm sorry for losing my cool back there and snapping at you guys."

"Hey, don't worry about it. Even JT blows her top sometimes." Micky looked up and tapped her chin. "Well, at least once."

"Just once." JT flashed Izzy a half smile. "Go on."

"It's something Bethany said that I never really thought about before." Izzy kept his head down and let out a breath. "Maybe it's a dumb question or maybe I should know the answer already, but it made me realize that I haven't studied the Bible as much as I thought I had. I know Genesis pretty well, but that's about it."

"That's okay. I've been studying it a lot longer than you, but I still ask my dad stuff all the time."

"And I'm always asking her questions about it," Micky said. "It's nothing to be embarrassed over. Even genius valedictorians don't know everything."

As Izzy looked up and chuckled, his eyes brightened. "Thanks. Okay, you know how the Old Testament has all those laws, right?"

JT nodded. "Sure."

"So there are a bunch of really strange ones. Like one of them says that a person isn't allowed to wear clothing made with two different types of fabrics. And another one forbids people from eating crab or lobster. The Bible even calls this an abomination." Izzy furrowed his brow. "So how come we don't follow those laws?"

"I don't eat shellfish." Jax stuck out his tongue and shook his head. "Blech."

Izzy ignored him and looked at JT, waiting for her to answer.

"That's a good question, and I can definitely picture Bethany using it." She looked up at the ceiling for a moment, thinking. "You might get different answers depending on what church you go to."

"What do you mean?" Izzy asked.

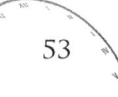

"Well, certain denominations have different ways of looking at the relationship between the Old and New Testaments, or to be more specific, the relationship between Israel and the Church. So, even though most Christians don't follow those laws, they reach that conclusion in different ways."

"What does our church teach?" Izzy asked.

"Our statement of faith teaches that Israel and the Church are separate entities. Because of that, Pastor would say that those laws were given to a specific people, the Israelites, at a specific place and time."

"So, because we're not Jews, we aren't under those laws?" Izzy tilted his head and licked his lips.

"Yep. God gave them to Israel right after He used Moses to lead them out of Egypt. They were supposed to teach those laws to their children. Our church believes that we are not under that covenant God made with Moses and the Israelites." JT squinted as she tried to think of an example. "It's kind of like how we follow the laws of the United States, when we aren't stuck in the past, because we're citizens of that country. We don't follow the laws of another country, like Brazil, because we aren't under those laws. When Jesus came, He established a new covenant, and we are part of that."

"That makes sense."

"And doesn't the New Testament specifically say that we're not under the law?" Jax asked.

"It sure does." JT closed her eyes as she tried to remember particular verses. "I know Paul wrote that to the Romans. Oh, and he told the Galatians that if they walk in the Spirit, then they are not under the law. In fact, this issue comes up a lot in the New Testament. Many of the churches the apostles wrote to were trying to figure out whether Gentile Christians were required to keep the law of Moses. And in Acts 15, some of the leading apostles got together in Jerusalem and agreed that the Gentile believers were not obligated to follow the old covenant, because they were under a new covenant."

Jax tapped the windshield menu to bring up a display of the battery's power gauge. "So Bethany's claim is just another in a long line of objections to the Bible that are based on misunderstandings of what it actually teaches."

Izzy adjusted his glasses. "Okay, but why would God give such strange laws in the first place?"

"Yeah, that's what I'm wondering," Micky said. "I kind of understand some of the dietary rules, but the fabric thing does sound pretty weird."

"I don't know all the reasons behind each specific law because God doesn't always tell us. Even though lots of people try to speculate, I think the main reason is that God didn't want the Israelites to be like the nations around them." JT stifled a yawn. "He repeatedly stressed that."

"While it's interesting to search for answers to things like this, I bet those laws didn't seem strange to the people at that time." Jax held up a hand. "I mean, it all probably made sense in light of their cultural setting. I'm sure they'd find some of our laws confusing too."

"Someone once told me that in Alabama it's illegal to carry an ice cream cone in your back pocket." Micky giggled as her friends stared at her in disbelief. "That sounded pretty ridiculous until I read that it was about the cone itself and had nothing to do with the ice cream."

Jax laughed and shook his head. "What are you talking about? Are you delirious?"

"Thanks for making my point, Thompson. While it sounds super crazy to us now, it turns out horse thieves used to put the sugary treats in their back pockets to entice a horse to follow them. That way if they got caught, they could say that they didn't steal the horse because it just followed them home."

"That actually makes sense," JT said. "I have an aunt back in Wisconsin who makes treats out of ice cream cones for her horses. So sometimes laws are based on the cultural needs of specific people at a specific time, and we might not always understand them."

"I could see that." Izzy looked at JT as if he wanted to ask something else, but then he turned to Jax. "How far are we from where we saw that T-rex?"

"I think it's a couple hours." Jax stared at the windshield. "I hope we still have some light left when we get there."

 Five

"Are you sure this is the place?" Micky asked.

Jax scanned the broad field before them. The faint trail they had been following entered a sub-tropical forest several hundred yards in the distance. "I think so. There weren't any other woodlands along the way, so it must be around here."

"Right." JT pointed past Izzy. "The caravan stopped on this side, and the T. rex approached from over there." She shifted her arm to the left.

"Maybe they came back for the arrows," Izzy said. "I'd guess things like that are fairly valuable to people at this time."

"That seems pretty risky," JT said.

"I agree, but maybe not for them." Izzy set the piece of sandstone on the floor. Over the past two hours, he had managed to bore a three-inch hole into the rock by turning a drill bit with his hands. "The rex couldn't keep up with the horse. So maybe one of the riders came back to collect the arrows."

Jax yawned for what seemed to be the hundredth time since they left the oasis. "Yeah, maybe. We should still look around for a few minutes, and if we don't find anything, then we'll get going. It's going to be dark in about an hour."

"Do you think we should try to find a safe place to stay?" JT asked. "I'm sure we could all use some sleep, and it's not like we'll have enough power to hover through the night."

Jax thought about a steep hill that they had passed while the girls had been fast asleep. "There was a pretty good spot about ten minutes ago, but I'd prefer to reach the other side of the forest first. Remember, if this is the right spot, then that T. rex was roaming around here yesterday."

JT stiffened and glanced behind them. "Maybe we should elevate a little higher."

Jax grinned as he remembered how scared JT had been upon seeing the T. rex, while he and Izzy had been awestruck. "Relax. I think we'd hear it before it ever got close. Besides, it can't really see us."

For the next several minutes, they hovered slowly over the area of the field where the arrows had probably landed. At JT's request, Jax significantly boosted the exterior microphone. Much to their relief, no earth-pounding footsteps or ear-splitting roars registered.

Izzy yawned. "I don't think we're going to find anything. I'll bet someone came back for them."

As if it were contagious, Jax yawned while checking the power meter. "So are you guys up for getting through the forest tonight, or at least a good chunk of it?"

"That depends. Can you stay awake that long?" Micky asked.

"Yeah, as long as someone else stays up to talk to me," Jax said.

"I will," Micky said. "I've already had a few naps."

"I can too." JT rubbed her eyes.

Izzy stretched his fingers and picked up the mold. "I'll keep working on this."

JT pointed at the large stone in Izzy's lap. "We can help with that."

"Thanks, but I don't mind. It gives me something to do."

"Okay, just let us know if you change your mind."

Jax turned the car toward the point where the trail entered the forest. "Looks like I'll have plenty of company." He activated the voice command. "Elevate to twenty feet."

JT placed her hand on Jax's shoulder. "Thank you."

"Twenty?" Micky asked.

"You didn't see that T. rex."

Jax carefully guided the car into the woods. Trees with giant broad leaves reached at least fifty feet in the air. He had little trouble maneuvering through the first hundred yards but decelerated to a walking speed as the forest became denser. Mindful of the multi-camera and solar panels on top of the vehicle, Jax regularly adjusted their height to keep a safe distance from the lower branches.

"Wouldn't it be easier to hover above the forest?" JT asked.

"I thought about doing that," Jax said. "It would drain the battery faster, but I guess it could also charge a little at the same time if we were out of all this shade."

Izzy grunted as he struggled to turn the drill bit further into the stone. "And we could speed up."

Jax scanned the treetops. "Okay, look for an opening in the canopy then." As he spoke, a low moan came through the speakers.

"What was that?" JT trembled as she bit her lip.

"I don't know." Jax spun around, checking their surroundings.

Another moan, followed by a high-pitched squeak filled the car. Jax stopped the vehicle and the four teens sat quietly, searching for the source. As the eerie sounds grew louder, a light thumping of footsteps joined the cacophony.

Micky jolted and pointed ahead. "Look!"

Jax leaned forward and squinted until two massive creatures with relatively small heads stepped into view. Huge bony plates jutted out of their backs, the tallest reaching over twelve feet in the air. The tail on each beast boasted two pairs of spikes and swayed side to side.

JT gripped Jax's shoulder. "Stegosaurs! Two of them."

The magnificent beasts lumbered by, oblivious to the four humans in the virtually invisible hovering vehicle.

"Not just two." Izzy pointed toward Jax's window. "Check it out."

Jax shifted to look, and his jaw dropped as nearly a dozen more stegosaurs marched toward them with three juveniles in the middle of the procession. Movement to his left grabbed Jax's attention, but it was only the branch closest to him shaking as the dinosaurs paraded below.

"They're so amazing," JT said. "Look at those little ones."

Micky cooed. "So cute."

Jax studied the nearest adult while it moved in front of them. Its shoulder muscles bulged and rippled with every step, and the enormous plates shifted back and forth. "That thing's got to be about the size of an elephant."

"Yeah," Izzy said. "Well, maybe not quite as tall, unless you count the plates. But definitely longer."

When the second-to-last dinosaur crossed their path, it stopped and stared in their direction.

JT leaned in and spoke softly. "Does it hear us?"

Jax shook his head. "I doubt it."

The stegosaur moaned loudly and then clumsily hurtled forward, triggering a stampede. Jax turned the exterior microphone down to fifty percent. "Um, why are they running?"

"Did it see us?" Micky asked.

"We're cloaked."

The words had scarcely left Jax's mouth when a deafening roar seemed to shake the car. Instinctively, the teens covered their ears. Jax had heard that sound before. Time seemed to slow as thunderous footsteps approached and the trees around them shook.

JT gasped. "T. rex!"

The creature charged toward them and, without conscious thought, Jax squeezed the voice-command button. "Elevate to twenty-five feet."

The forest trembled as the massive beast stomped past them on the way to the stegosaurs. Suddenly, the car jolted and leaves rained down around them. Something blocked the multi-camera, leaving the teens blind to anything outside. The driver's side ceased to elevate while the other side continued to rise.

"What was that?" Izzy grabbed the door to stop himself from sliding into Jax.

"I think we hit a branch," Jax said as he worked to straighten the vehicle.

The limb creaked as the car pushed against it. Before Jax could react, the branch snapped and scraped its way down his side of the car, taking the camera-blocking leaf with it. As the car leveled out and their surroundings appeared again, Jax realized he no longer heard the massive footsteps. He spun to look out Izzy's window, searching for the T. rex.

Izzy froze and his eyes grew wide as Micky stifled a scream.

JT gripped his shoulder so tightly that her nails dug into his skin. "It's looking right at us."

Moving nothing but his mouth, Jax spoke softly. "Shh. We're still cloaked."

The tyrannosaur lowered its head when another branch hit the ground. After considering the object for a few seconds, the monster sniffed the air and looked directly at them again.

"Then why is it staring at us?" Micky asked through clenched teeth.

"I don't know." Jax swallowed the lump in his throat. "Maybe it can smell us."

"But it can't reach us, right?" JT asked.

Jax's eyes shifted to the power meter. "Not yet, but it will soon. We're running out of juice."

The titanic predator bent low and opened its huge jaw, displaying two rows of deadly daggers. Suddenly, it unleashed the loudest roar Jax had ever heard, causing him to white-knuckle the steering wheel. After five seconds of ear-splitting horror, the beast tilted its head and continued studying them.

"C'mon, look away," Izzy said under his breath.

A small wooden shaft near the dinosaur's snout caught Jax's eye. "I'll bet that's the same one we saw before. I think that's part of an arrow in its right nostril."

"I see it," Izzy said. "Now, let's hope he can't see us."

Jax chanced a quick look at the power readout again, and his stomach clenched when he noticed a blinking light. "Um, guys. Don't react, no matter what." He let out a short breath and tried to keep his voice calm. "It *can* see us. I'm not sure what happened, but the cloak is malfunctioning." He squeezed the button. "Engage cloak."

The car's computerized voice responded. *"Error. Cannot engage cloak at this time."*

"What are we going to do?" JT's grip on his shoulder tightened even more, and Jax fought the urge to express his discomfort.

"We have to get out of here." Jax mentally focused on the path they had taken to this point, trying to remember the lowest they traveled. He gulped when he recalled a few instances where they had dipped below fifteen feet. "If we stay above twenty feet, it shouldn't be able to reach us."

"How fast can we go?" Micky asked.

"We estimated about thirty miles per hour," Izzy said. "But that's out in the open when we aren't dodging trees."

"And how fast can it go?" She slowly lifted her finger to point toward the brute below.

"Hopefully, not thirty," JT said.

Izzy rubbed his palms on his pants. "The studies I've read claim that it probably couldn't top fifteen, even though movies show it going a lot faster."

"There's one way to find out." Jax stretched his fingers to allow the blood to circulate through them once again. "I'll be focusing on the branches. Iz, you need to look for a clearing in the canopy that we can elevate through to try to lose him. JT and Micky, keep an eye on that thing and tell me if it gets too close. Oh, you should probably pray, too."

Each of the teens quietly agreed to his plan, and JT's lips started moving in what Jax assumed was silent prayer.

"Okay, I'm going to lay on the horn to see if we can confuse it for a few seconds. Then I need to spin us around and take off the way we came." Jax closed his eyes and took a deep breath. *Lord, please keep us safe.*

He glanced at the power level again and estimated that they had fifteen minutes before they dropped out of the sky. "Everyone ready?"

"Just don't go too low," Izzy said. "If he gets close, we can always move up into the branches again."

Jax nodded.

"Be careful," JT said.

Jax sucked in a deep breath, steeling himself for danger and focusing entirely on the task ahead. "Here we go." He slammed on the horn and held it down while simultaneously dropping a few feet. As the tyrannosaur reared back and shook its head, Jax spun the car 180 degrees. After thrusting forward, he descended to dodge a branch and his eyes flashed to the altitude on the windshield. *Seventeen feet.* The T. rex lumbered behind them in pursuit, getting closer by the second, with each step resounding through the forest.

"Go, go, go." Micky slapped Izzy's seat.

Biting his lip and with a quick glance to the rearview, Jax moved them lower to dodge another limb. JT screamed as the T. rex lunged forward in an attempt to bite the rear of the car, but its teeth snapped only air, missing by what seemed inches.

Jax elevated again and pushed the hover devices to full throttle. The car sped forward, putting a bit of distance between them and the charging dinosaur. "Any clearing yet?"

Izzy continued to peer up through the windshield. "Nothing."

"Okay." Jax swerved to the left and down a couple of feet. "We shouldn't be too far from where it thins out." He veered back to the right and over a low-lying limb, which shattered a few seconds later when the beast crashed through it.

"Hurry up!" JT said.

"I'm trying." Branches from a trio of trees blocked their path a short distance ahead. "How far back is he?"

"About thirty feet," Micky said.

"Okay, hold on." With one last check of the rearview, Jax slowed the car slightly and descended to eight feet to duck under the numerous obstructions.

Micky rapidly tapped the center console. "What are you doing?"

JT shook Jax's seat. "Hurry!"

Jax glanced in his side mirror. The T. rex drew closer with every massive stride, but then slowed as it neared the muddled limbs. It turned to the left to go around the blockade, which allowed the teens to increase their lead.

After they passed under the barrier, the trees thinned, and Jax jammed the throttle to raise the car to twenty feet.

"It's slowing down." JT stared out the back window. The dinosaur bellowed again, causing her to wince. She sighed loudly and Jax saw her shoulders relax. "It stopped."

Jax had lost the trail during the chase. He estimated it was a little to their right, so he drifted in that direction as they hovered through the patchwork of trees. When he saw the field in front of them, he finally let out a deep breath. "Whew. That was too close."

JT closed her eyes and leaned back. "It's always too close."

Izzy slapped him on the knee. "Nice flyin' man. Wanna do it again?"

Jax allowed a nervous chuckle to escape his mouth. "Maybe tomorrow."

"Well, we might have to." Izzy gestured to the outside of the vehicle. "If we can't figure out what's wrong with the cloak, we won't be able to hide from things like that."

The long shadows of the trees stretched across much of the field as the sun dipped low in the western sky. After checking for danger, Jax lowered the vehicle to a few feet above the ground to conserve power. "I'm going to try to reach that hill I saw earlier. It should be a few miles ahead. Hopefully, it'll be a safe place to stay the night."

SIX
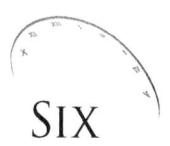

"That's about as far as we're going to get." Jax's eyes flicked from the altitude readout to the front of the car as they landed on the ground with a slight bump. He cut power to the hover devices and allowed the car's normal battery to take over for the computer and dash controls.

"Do you think it can find us here?" Micky asked.

Izzy shrugged. "I doubt it's even looking. Maybe it decided to go after those stegosauruses."

"Plus, the battery lasted longer than I expected. We might've gone about ten miles." Jax looked out toward the vast plain and could barely see the distant forest in the faint light. "And we're way up on this steep hill."

JT twisted as she stretched her arms and yawned. "I hope there aren't any other dangers out here."

"Me too." Izzy pointed to the clock. "It's already 6:00 in the morning back home. We should probably get some sleep."

"Not yet." Jax stared at the blinking error message. "We've gotta figure out what happened to the cloak."

"Can't it wait until morning?" Izzy asked.

"It could," Jax said. "But I'd rather do it now

so we can be thinking about how to repair it, if possible."

Jax, JT, and Izzy climbed out of the car, and Jax closed the door, taking in a breath of the humid air. With the help of his phone's flashlight feature, he checked the roof and then winced at the sizeable dent and corresponding scratch in the paint. "My dad's not gonna be happy." *If we ever make it back home, that is.* He panned down the outside of the door and groaned when he spotted an empty socket where a cloaking rod should have been.

Izzy came around the front of the car. "What's wrong?"

Jax pointed to the middle of the door. "That's why the cloak malfunctioned."

"Yeah, that would do it." Izzy rubbed the back of his neck.

"So if just one of those little posts is missing, the whole cloak goes down?" JT asked.

"That's right," Izzy said.

JT forced a smile. "Sounds like a design flaw to me."

Jax snickered, thankful for a moment of levity in a day that had gone from bad to worse.

"Can it be repaired?" she asked as Micky joined them.

Jax bent down and examined the slot where the rod should have been. "Seems okay. We just need to find the piece and snap it back in."

JT waved her hands and shook her head. "Whoa, are you saying that we need to go back there?"

"I'm with JT." Micky's eyes were wide. "That does *not* sound like a good idea."

"We don't really have a choice." Jax stared back in the direction of the forest. "We can't cloak without it and we can't leave that rod in the past for someone to find."

"They wouldn't even know what it is," Micky leaned against the car and folded her arms across her chest.

"That's true, but we'd still risk changing things." Jax held up his phone. "Imagine if ancient people found advanced technology and ended up inventing all sorts of things they never would've dreamed of otherwise." He looked at Izzy and snapped his fingers. "What was that time travel movie where that happened?"

Izzy shrugged. "We watched so many of them."

The girls both rolled their eyes and JT giggled.

Izzy hopped up on the hood. "Even if that's not an issue, we'll definitely want that cloak working in case we need to find out if those people worked with silver."

JT pressed her fingertips to her forehead and released a tired breath. "But how are we going to avoid the T. rex? We've seen it in that forest both times we've been there."

Jax raised his palms. "Well, best case scenario is that we swoop in there tomorrow morning and leave without the rex ever knowing we were there."

"When have we ever been that lucky?" Micky asked. "We should plan for the worst."

"I agree." Jax stroked his chin. "But before we go anywhere, we should fully charge the battery in the morning."

"Yeah, but how do we retrieve that rod if the T. rex is there?" JT asked.

Over the next half-hour, they brainstormed about potential plans before narrowing it down to a few options. A final decision would be reached when they arrived on the scene.

With the rudiments of a plan in place, the four fell silent, listening to the sounds of the settling night. Jax reclined on the hood next to Izzy and stared up at the stars, shining bright in a cloudless sky. "This sort of reminds me of our first trip."

"Seriously?" Micky asked.

"Well, we were chased by a large dinosaur, ran out of power, and had to spend the night on a hillside."

"Only this time it's much more dangerous." JT sat on the hood and rested her back against the windshield. "That T. rex is much bigger than Al, the car is broken, and we probably need to put ourselves in harm's way again."

The car rocked slightly as Micky hoisted herself onto the trunk. She scooted up the back window and sprawled on the roof, with her head toward the front.

Jax bit into a piece of fruit. "True, but that'll just make it more memorable when we get home."

"*If* we get home," Izzy said.

Even with all the obstacles standing in their way, Jax wanted to keep their spirits up. "We'll be fine. You'll see. Just like the first trip."

"You know what else is like our first trip?" Micky waited for an answer, but when no one spoke, she said, "We're all laying out looking at the stars."

"Oh yeah." JT smiled down at Jax and then glanced at Izzy and Micky. "Although this time I don't have to try to convince you that we aren't millions of years in the past."

Micky laughed. "No, you sure don't. But this reminds me of something I read in Dr. Chiler's book."

JT let out a mock groan. "Oh, here we go again."

"Hey, I haven't mentioned her since we got here."

JT giggled. "I know. I'm just teasing. Go ahead."

"Yeah, I want to hear it," Izzy said.

Jax pulled his knees up and rested his feet on the front of the hood. "Me too."

"Well, most of her book was like an expansion of her talk about how so many of the details from Genesis 1–11 can be found in the legends of ancient people groups." Micky folded her hands and slipped them under her head like a pillow. "But she also has a section of the book that focuses on constellations."

"Constellations?" Izzy asked. "Why?"

"She said that the constellations and the stories attached to some of them provide additional evidence that the early peoples shared a common history." Micky raised an arm and pointed to the sky. "There's the Big Dipper, which we all know is part of Ursa Major, the Great Bear. But do you actually see anything that resembles a bear?"

Jax followed the familiar stars, knowing that the "handle" formed the bear's tail. Then he tried unsuccessfully to locate other stars that would provide the outline for the body, head, and legs of the Great Bear. "No. It's way too subjective. There are too many bright stars in that part of the sky. You could draw lines just about anywhere."

"I guess if you knew which stars to connect, you could see it as a bear," Izzy said.

Micky lowered her arm. "Exactly. You might be able to explain why Native American tribes like the Cherokee, Iroquois, and Zuni call it a bear. Maybe they learned that idea from each other. But why do so many people from the Old World, like the Greeks, Hebrews, and Basques also call it a bear?"

"The Hebrews?" JT asked. "Oh yeah, the Old Testament mentions it, right?

"Yes, it's in the book of Job twice," Micky said.

Jax rubbed his tired eyes. "That's very interesting. It's not like they were communicating across the oceans about what people should call the constellations."

"So is Dr. Chiler suggesting that the people at Babel called it a bear and then when they split up, they took that idea with them and passed it down generation after generation?" Izzy asked.

"Yep, but not just because of Ursa Major." Micky rolled onto her stomach and pushed her ponytail behind her. "Did you know that Homer and Hesiod mentioned the Pleiades star cluster? In Greek mythology, they're known as the Seven Sisters, daughters of the titan Atlas."

"Yeah, I knew that," JT said.

"Well, it's generally believed that the Greeks borrowed their constellations from the Mesopotamians at least a century after Hesiod, so why would they call it the same thing as people all around the globe?" Micky opened the book and used the light from her phone as she flipped through several pages. "All the following groups refer to the Pleiades as the Seven Sisters: the Nez Perce of the northwest United States, the Monte Alto of Guatemala, the Ban Raji of northern India, and the Worrora and Wurundjeri peoples of Australia." She closed the book, keeping a finger in as a bookmark. "It makes sense to think of them as seven of something, since there are seven bright stars in the cluster. But why do so many call them sisters?"

"Does she talk about there being any other explanations?" Jax asked.

"Yeah, she says the primary view is that it's just coincidental."

"That's really a huge stretch," Izzy said.

"True," Micky said. "But it's not like secular researchers are going to say, 'Oh, I'll bet that Babel event in Genesis 11 is the best explanation.'"

"No, it couldn't possibly be what the Bible says," JT said, her voice full of sarcasm.

"Usually, the people who argue for coincidence point to some of the ones that actually look like the thing they are named after." Micky took a deep breath. "Dr. Chiler talked about her favorite one, the Southern Cross. It's the one on the flags of Brazil, New Zealand, and of course, her home country of Australia. And it's easy to see the shape of a cross in it."

JT chuckled. "I think it looks like a kite, because there's no star in the middle to cross the lines."

"Yeah, she always thought that too," Micky said. "It's well-known in the Southern Hemisphere, but there are even some ancient peoples in the lower latitudes of the Northern Hemisphere who called it a cross."

"How could they see it?" Jax asked. "Isn't it just a constellation in the Southern Hemisphere?"

"I'll bet that they would've been able to see it thousands of years ago because of axial precession," Izzy said.

"Oh yeah." Jax remembered from astronomy class that the term referred to the gradual shift in the orientation of Earth's axis.

"That's right." Micky looked at the sky for a moment and then pointed toward the horizon. "Orion is another one. Well, it's not hard to imagine those stars in the shape of a giant man, so it's not surprising to find several cultures who refer to that constellation as a giant or a hunter. But again, the coincidence theory doesn't explain all the ones that really don't look like what they represent."

"I think the Babel explanation makes perfect sense," Izzy said. "Although, I suppose someone could say that people got these ideas from trading between ancient groups."

"Yeah, that's another common view." Micky cracked a knuckle. "But it doesn't really account for the indigenous Australians or Native Americans."

Jax suppressed a yawn. He suddenly felt extremely tired. He closed his eyes as he rolled onto his side.

"What about the stories attached to the constellations?" JT asked. "Did she say anything about them having a basis in reality? I don't mean the Great Bear, but what about Orion being a giant man or some of the others?"

Jax repositioned his arm underneath his head to get comfortable.

"Yeah, she has a section about how some of those stories might date back to Babel or even before that."

Izzy said something, but it sounded like he was mumbling under water. The next thing Jax knew, JT shook his shoulder. "Wake up."

"Hm?"

She squeezed his arm and then let go. "We're all going to sleep in the car."

"Already?" Jax asked.

JT giggled. "You've been asleep for over half an hour."

 Seven

What a crazy dream! The thoughts of the time machine breaking down in the past and being chased by a tyrannosaurus flashed into his mind as Izzy stretched his arm out. When his hand hit the passenger window, his eyes shot open. He blinked several times and sat up straight. As the morning sunlight streamed through the windshield, Izzy grabbed his glasses from the dashboard and put them on. He was all alone in Jax's father's time machine. *Oh no, it wasn't a dream. We're really stuck here.*

He opened the door and stepped out into warmer-than-expected air. Taking a deep breath, Izzy stretched his arms above his head and looked around. Jax, JT, and Micky were a little farther up the hill facing the forest. Izzy made sure his door was unlocked before closing it and walked slowly and stiffly toward the others. Far below, the grassy plain stretched for miles, dotted by occasional patches of trees.

Jax turned and grinned. "Look who's up."

"Good morning, Izzy," JT said.

Izzy shook his hands as if it would help him wake up. "Mornin'."

Micky glanced at her watch. "About time."

"How long have you guys been up?"

"About an hour for me." Jax tipped his head toward the girls. "Fifteen minutes for them."

"Did they explain our latest plan if the rex is there?" Izzy asked.

Jax nodded slowly. "Yeah, it's a good backup plan, but there's one change. I'm doing it."

Izzy had anticipated that Jax would insist on putting himself in the greatest danger. "I appreciate that, but I'm doing it." Jax opened his mouth to object, but Izzy cut him off. "No, I'm doing it, and that's final. We need you to fly the vehicle."

"Well, hopefully it won't come to that," JT said.

"Right." Jax shot JT a mischievous smile. "Although it'd be kind of cool to get a better look at that rex in the daylight."

JT returned his look with an expressionless stare. "No, it wouldn't."

Micky laughed and nudged JT. "He's kidding."

"How long until the battery's ready?" Izzy asked.

"Probably another hour." Jax pointed toward the car. "We'll want to make sure the repulsors are secured and that everything else is working before we leave."

"Okay." Micky waved a hand toward JT. "C'mon, girl. Let's check those since we invented them."

Izzy stared out across the plain until Jax

stepped into his view. "About that plan."

Izzy shook his head. "Listen. It makes sense for me to do it because it's my fault that we're stuck here and I want to make amends. But we also need you to do your fancy flying to lure that thing away if it comes to that. JT could probably do my part because she's the best climber, but we both know that you'd never agree to that."

Jax scratched the back of his neck. "But I don't want anything to happen to any of you."

Izzy brushed his foot over the grass as he breathed in the crisp morning air. "This is gonna sound a little cheesy, but hear me out." He looked up at Jax. "You're the glue that holds our group together. We all look up to you—and not just the three of us; our whole school does. And you're always willing to risk your life for us."

Jax blinked hard and turned his head away. "Thanks. I don't think about it like that. I'm just trying to do the right thing."

"I know." Izzy swallowed a lump in his throat. "And I remember back when you really only focused on what you wanted, but even then, you were the bravest person I knew. You came back for me when I was hiding from Al in the tree. But since you became a Christian, I can tell that you really care about us more than yourself."

Jax breathed deeply. "I really appreciate that, but why are you telling me this now?"

"Because I may not have a chance after today."
"We'll be fine."

"I wish I had your confidence." Izzy sighed and turned his head. "About everything."

Jax cupped Izzy's shoulder. "You doin' alright?"

Izzy's shoes suddenly became very interesting as he studied them.

"It's something Bethany said, isn't it? You shouldn't let her get to you. She just wants to attack our faith, so she'll say anything, no matter how crazy it is."

"I know." Izzy slowly lifted his head. "But what if she's right? Not about creation or evolution. I don't have any doubts about that." He swept an arm in the direction of the forest. "I can see that for myself. But this time was different. She was going after Jesus. How do we know we can trust everything the Bible says about Him? I guess I always took it for granted that if I could trust the beginning of the Bible, then I could trust the rest of it." He bit his lip. "But that isn't logical."

Jax ran his fingers through his spikey blue and black hair. "No, I guess it isn't. It does remove a large objection from skeptics, though."

"It does. But if the Gospels were written a century after Jesus lived and no contemporary historians wrote about Him, can we really trust what we read?" He lifted his palms and shrugged. "What if the most important ideas about Jesus really were copied from pagan gods like she said, or if He wasn't considered to be divine until the fourth century? Can we really claim that Christianity is true?"

Jax stuffed his hands into his front pockets. "Have you looked into any of those things yet?"

He shook his head. "I've been too busy ever since it happened. I was going to ask Pastor Rich, but Dr. Chiler was there. And then we went to that conference, where I was focused on answering Mei-Lin's question about the animals on the Ark. And now this."

Jax pushed his lips to the side. "Maybe JT knows about some books on those things, or maybe she's has already studied them. We can ask her."

"That sounds good." Izzy grabbed Jax's arm as he started walking toward the car. "Please don't tell the girls that I've been having some doubts. I don't want them to worry about me. We can just ask how she'd answer those challenges."

"Okay. But you know JT wouldn't think any less of you. You saw how she handled the one about those strange laws in the Old Testament."

"I know."

"She put up with my anger and doubts for a long time." Jax's eyes widened. "Hey, she once challenged me not to get mad at God about what happened to my dad or anything else unless I first checked to see if there were good answers." Jax put a hand on Izzy's shoulder. "We should make the same deal. There's no reason for you to have doubts about the faith just because Bethany made some claims. Look into them before allowing doubts to creep in. I'm sure there are good answers. And we'll all help out. Deal?"

"Uh, yeah. Deal." Izzy forced an unconvincing half smile. "Thanks."

* * *

Izzy stared wide-eyed at two thick broken branches while the hovering car floated past them. "Those must be the limbs the T. rex destroyed while chasing us."

"Looks like it," Jax said. "The part should be just a little farther ahead. Look for the branch that we hit."

A few seconds later, Micky pointed past Jax. "I think that's it. On the ground dead ahead."

Izzy glanced at the downed limb and then at the tree. "She's right. Stop right next to it, and I'll find the part."

Jax tapped a few controls and the car slowed and descended.

"Wait. Any sign of the T. rex?" JT asked.

The teens looked around in every direction, and Jax cranked up the exterior microphone's volume. After several quiet moments, Jax shook his head. "Looks clear to me."

"Me too," Izzy said. "Let's make this quick."

After Jax lowered the car to a few inches above the ground next to the branch, Izzy opened his door and hopped out. Silence filled the warm air and sunlight streamed through tiny openings in the canopy, dappling the forest floor. As Izzy stepped around the open door, the trees in front of him shook violently and the sound of cracking wood reverberated through the small clearing.

The T. rex's massive head protruded through a gap in the trees just as Izzy darted back around the door and dove into his seat. "Go!"

JT screamed and Micky gripped Izzy's headrest.

"Elevate twenty-five feet!" Jax grabbed Izzy's arm as the car shot upward. "Close the door."

Izzy righted himself only to see the dinosaur charging at them, filling up more of his view with each step. Its huge jaw opened, flaunting rows of sharp teeth. *We're not going to make it!* "Back up."

"Working on it." Jax winced and stiffened his arms and legs as if bracing for impact.

Izzy held his breath as the car continued to elevate and the T. rex disappeared from sight. Following a few tense seconds, Izzy peeked out of his open door. The giant beast stood a few feet below and in front of them. Its relatively small arms waved in the air as a roar blasted through the forest and echoed in the car. He closed his door and faced Jax. "It can't reach us."

"We should get out of here," Micky said.

"No, wait." Jax appeared to be studying something outside of his window. "This could work." He gestured toward a nearby tree and slowly spun the car so that Izzy could see it. "What do you think?"

Izzy scanned the tree, paying close attention to the distance between the branches and the thickness of the trunk. He swallowed a lump in his throat and let out a breath. "Yeah, let's do it."

"Let's come back later." JT's voice quivered.

"Or just leave it," Micky said.

Izzy shook his head and took a couple breaths to slow his heartrate. "No, we need that part. Don't worry. It'll be fine." He pushed one of his earphones into place and cleared his throat. "Can you hear me?"

"Yeah, I've got you." Jax jolted and tapped a few times on his phone's screen. "Hold on … there it is … just a couple more seconds … okay. Now say something."

"What were you doing?" Izzy asked just before hearing his own question repeated through the car's speakers.

"Now, we'll all be able to hear you, although I think it's still just using my mic," Jax said.

Izzy nodded "It is. I heard you through the earbud. Let's do this."

Jax carefully nestled the passenger side of the car up close to the tree as Izzy guided him. "How's that?"

"Good." Izzy checked the rope they had wound around part of his seat's base. It extended ten feet and ended in a small loop to make it easier to grasp. "I don't think I'll need this rope right now."

"Just hang onto it until you're secure," JT said.

"Okay. Here I go."

JT placed a hand on his shoulder. "Be careful."

"Yeah, be safe," Micky said.

"You sure you don't want to switch places?" Jax asked.

Izzy let out a small laugh and then took a deep breath. "No, I got this."

"Okay, let us know when you find it and we'll pick you up." Jax gave him a grim nod. "Don't climb down until we lead that thing far away."

"Definitely. Don't let it get too close." Izzy picked up the end of the rope and pushed his torso through the open window. He lifted one leg through so that he straddled the door. Then he grabbed the limb above his head and tugged on it to make sure it could support his weight. Holding tightly to the rope and branch, he slid out of the window and stepped on another limb beneath him. Izzy tossed the rope back into the vehicle.

He maneuvered his way around to a branch on the opposite side of the trunk and pressed himself against it. "All set."

Jax's voice came through the earbud. "Alright, hold on tight. Now it's our turn."

The tree shook as the T. rex roared, and Izzy tightened his grip. He waited a few seconds to peek around the trunk. The time machine dipped slightly and picked up speed with the dinosaur following close behind, its pounding footsteps forcing Izzy to wince.

"It's working," Jax said.

Izzy kept his voice low and climbed to the branch beneath him. "Don't slow down."

The vehicle sank lower but remained out of range of the rampaging rex. When both disappeared from sight and the footsteps could barely be heard, Izzy scrambled down the tree, being careful not to slip and injure himself.

Upon reaching the ground, he sprinted to the downed branch and dragged it aside. He scanned the area, but nothing metallic stood out. *Come on, hurry up, Iz.* He double-checked the newly uncovered patch of soil but to no avail. *Maybe it's caught in the leaves.* He spun around and flipped over the broken limb. A small reflection of light caught his attention and he hurried to the other end. While digging through the foliage, his hand brushed against the coolness of the metal rod.

Thank You, Lord.

As he reached for the part, his earphone crackled. "... ing ba ..."

"What?" Izzy asked as he picked up the rod and stood.

"... coming ... get ... of there!"

Izzy looked up and realized the footsteps were growing louder. He dashed back to the tree, shoved the thin end of the rod in his back pocket, and started climbing. His heart pounded nearly as loud as the monster's stomps.

"Are you back in the tree?" Jax asked.

Izzy grunted as he pulled himself upward, and he glimpsed movement to the left out of the corner of his eye. "Sort of."

The car's horn blared a short distance away and Jax shouted something out his window.

As Izzy attained the third branch, the footsteps reverberated through the tree, and he thought he could hear and feel the dinosaur's breath. He peeked over his shoulder and spotted the beast just seconds away, its eyes locked onto Izzy and its mouth open. Fear seized his heart, and his mind flashed back to the allosaurus that nearly killed him two years earlier. But the tyrannosaur was bigger, much bigger. Izzy glanced up to his destination. *I'll never make it.*

With no other option, he ducked under the limb in front of him, grabbed the cloaking rod in his left hand, and leapt from the tree. His legs buckled when he hit the ground, but he quickly regained his footing and ran. As a mighty roar blasted his eardrums, he flinched and almost dropped the metal piece. The cracking of branches and Jax's pleas to get to safety made him feel like he was running through quicksand. He glanced back again. The rex stepped past the tree and lumbered after him.

"Where are you guys?" Izzy gasped for air and searched for the car as he zigzagged through the woods, trying to prevent the dinosaur from using its long strides to catch him.

"Almost there," Jax said. "I see you."

Izzy dashed between two large trees that had grown close together, forcing the beast to go around.

"Turn to your left and keep running," Jax said. "We'll swoop down and get you."

His lungs screaming for air and leg muscles burning, Izzy veered left and slipped on some loose dirt. Pain shot up his back, but he leapt to his feet like a desperate rabbit as the dinosaur gained on him.

"Almost there," Jax said. "Micky, get ready to drop the rope."

Izzy looked over his shoulder as he sprinted toward a clearing. The car raced behind him, roughly ten feet in the air with the tyrannosaur in hot pursuit. "Hurry up!"

He broke through the trees and considered changing course when he heard Jax's voice again. "Drop it now!" The rope instantly appeared a few feet in front of him, the loop at the end nearly scraping the ground.

Izzy urged his throbbing legs to go faster as the beast unleashed a deafening bellow. He leaned forward and caught the swaying rope in his left hand. Being careful not to release the cloaking rod, he pulled the rope toward his body and gripped it with his right hand. "Got it!"

"Okay!"

Micky looked down at him from the open door. "Hold on, Izzy."

His fingers clenched the rope even tighter as the car rose and his feet left the ground. His stomach sank when the time machine tilted and lost elevation due to the extra weight on one side. The adrenaline racing through his system allowed him to pull himself up a bit. He lifted his foot to insert it into the loop but missed and ended up kicking it away from him. As it swung back, Izzy stopped it with his lower leg and then carefully placed his shoe into the loop. "Go!"

The T. rex lunged forward and snapped its menacing jaws at him, missing only by a couple of feet.

JT's scream rang out from the car and from

his earpiece.

"Hang on, Iz!" Jax said.

As they neared the edge of the clearing, Izzy closed his eyes and tightened his grip in preparation to crash into the fast-approaching foliage. But the car rose rapidly and sunlight struck his face. Soon the dinosaur was well below them and Izzy took a full breath. As he stared down at the creature, he was filled with a sense of awe and respect.

"How much longer can you hold on?" Micky yelled out the passenger window.

Izzy made sure his foot was securely in the loop and then looked up at her and smiled. "As long as I need to."

EIGHT

JT jumped out of the car and hugged Izzy. "Thank God you're safe. That was so scary."

"You're telling me." Izzy tossed the rope into the front seat and flexed his fingers. "I can't stop shaking."

"Come on, it was at least two or three feet away from you." Jax grinned. "Al knocked me off that ledge. If the rex touched you, then you'd have the right to be scared."

"I think maybe next time I'll let you do that part then." Izzy chuckled. "Plus, Al was a lot smaller."

"I know," Jax said. "So you're saying you don't want to do it again."

"No way."

"And I thought it was bad in the car." Micky shuddered. "That thing almost got us twice before it turned around and went after you."

"Ha! This coming from the only one of us who hasn't been chased by a dinosaur outside of the car."

"Oh, stop whining." Micky giggled and slapped Izzy's shoulder. "Maybe I'm just smart enough not to put myself in those situations."

"You might still have a chance." JT swept an arm to indicate the field around them. "Two days ago, that rex was right around here charging at those people."

"Well, there's no sign of it now." Jax stared at the forest roughly half a mile away. It appeared quiet for now. He closed his eyes and took in a deep breath. *Lord, thank You for protecting Izzy and the rest of us.* With a quick glance at the sky, he estimated it was probably early afternoon. "See, I told you everything would be fine."

JT playfully pushed his shoulder. "Always the optimist. I'm just glad you were right this time."

Jax laughed. "Well, I gotta be sooner or later."

Izzy handed him the cloaking rod. "Here you go."

Jax studied the metal piece. "Good work, Iz. We should pop this back in and get going."

"My thoughts exactly." Izzy looked around. "I'm not going to miss this area at all. Plus, I need to finish working on that mold for the wire."

Jax walked to his car door, squatted down, and snapped the rod back into place. He gripped it and gave it a slight shake. It held fast. "That wasn't too hard."

"Says you," Izzy said, grinning.

"Think it'll work?" JT asked as she stepped past Jax to climb in the back.

Jax shrugged. "Let's find out."

The teens piled into their customary seats, and JT handed around some fruit. Jax powered the car and triggered the speech-command button. "Engage cloak." The interior darkened, lit only by the electronics in the dash and a hint of dreary light that managed to penetrate the cloak like sunlight through the thickest fog. "Oh, I forgot. Engage multi-camera." Within a few seconds the windows displayed the scenery outside the car.

"Looks like it's working," Micky said.

"It'd better be after all I went through for it," Izzy said.

As he chewed on a bite of fruit, Jax raised the car a few feet off the ground and directed it back toward their destination. He checked the power gauge and made a few quick calculations. "I think we should try to stay above the forest as long as we can keep the trail in sight."

"Will we have enough power for that?" JT asked.

Jax caught her eye in the rearview mirror. "Depends on how high we'll be and how far we need to go. We should be able to hover for at least a couple of hours. Maybe longer if the sun stays out and keeps the panels charging."

"That sounds like a good plan to me then," JT said.

"Me too." Izzy picked up the sandstone mold and pushed the drill bit into the hole he had started on the opposite end from the one he bored the day before. Since the drill bit was not long enough to create one long tunnel through the rock, he planned to drill one hole from each side and have them meet in the middle.

"How's that coming along?" Jax asked.

Izzy shrugged. "It's not too bad. I just need to make sure I line up these two holes perfectly."

"And we need to find some silver," Jax said.

"And a way to melt it," Micky said.

JT leaned forward. "And avoid more dinosaur attacks."

"Sounds easy enough." Jax laughed, and as they rapidly approached the trees, he directed the car to rise about fifty feet.

For the next hour, the trail was fairly easy to follow, thanks to the caravan's sauropods and ankylosaurs. Plenty of tracks and broken branches led the way like a flashing road sign. Izzy continued working on the mold, and at JT's request, recounted all the details of his most recent terrifying encounter. Eventually, the conversation shifted to some of the wildlife in the forest below and guesses as to what lay on the other side.

"Those clouds ahead are getting pretty dark," Micky said. "Looks like we might be heading into some rain."

Izzy looked up from his work. "Sure does. We'll probably want to find a place to set down."

"It doesn't look too bad," Jax said.

Izzy pushed his glasses back into place. "Light

rain would be fine, but if it's a storm, then we could get caught in some strong winds."

"And lightning," JT said.

"Yeah, that'd be bad. Okay, look for a good spot to land." Jax glanced down at his phone and a thought struck him. "Hey, remember to make sure the phones, translator earbuds, and the sonic confusion devices are all fully charged."

"Will the translators have a longer range once we're out of the woods?" Micky asked.

"Maybe a little, but still around a quarter mile at best."

"That's it?" Micky shook her head. "We would've designed them to work for miles."

Jax snorted and rolled his eyes. "Of course, because I'm sure you could've expanded the phone's capabilities without wi-fi or mobile service."

"I guess we'll just never know." Micky tilted her head while she smirked.

"And what about our devices?" JT asked. "Do you really think we'll need them?"

Jax shrugged. "I hope not, but we may as well be prepared."

"Makes sense." After biting into a red fruit, JT wiped her mouth with the back of her hand. "I can't wait to get home and eat something other than these."

"Same here." Micky gestured toward the passenger window. "Hey, how does that look?"

In the distance, a sizeable creek flowing from a hilly region offered ample space to land on the opposite bank just outside the woods.

Suddenly, they swayed front to back and the girls gasped simultaneously. Fighting against the gusting wind, Jax angled the car downward into a gap in the trees, a refuge that offered shelter from the gale but provided very little protection from the rain.

"That's so strange." Jax studied the windshield and the slight discolorations in the screen where the water streaked down outside and interfered with the light coming through the display. "We can hear the rain and see it through the camera." Jax gestured toward the middle of the car's roof. "But the droplets don't show up on the windows because that's not the camera's point of view." He chuckled. "I don't even need to turn on the wipers when it's pouring."

"We probably should've anticipated that," Izzy said without looking up from the mold.

As the vehicle slowed and neared the ground, Jax considered a fairly level spot close to the brook. "Does this look safe?"

Izzy peered briefly in each direction. "Yeah. The trees will break some of the wind, and we won't be the tallest thing out here if there's lightning."

"Now what?" Micky asked as Jax brought the car to rest.

"Even though it's just a light rain right now, that storm is getting closer, and I think we should wait here until it passes us," Jax said.

"Look." Micky aimed a finger toward the passenger side of the windshield. "Is that another saber-tooth?"

A large catlike creature strode cautiously toward the water's edge. After stopping a few feet from the stream, it turned and stared in their direction. Two long fangs extended from its upper jaw, but they did not go beyond its lower jaw, which dropped a few inches to accommodate its long canine teeth. Its brown coat contrasted with the various greens of the subtropical forest and grays of the rainy day. The creature tilted its head and sniffed the air. Satisfied, it looked in the opposite direction before approaching the water to drink.

Keeping his voice low, Jax said, "I don't think so. It looks a lot different than the one Izzy and I saw up close last year. I bet it's one of those creatures Dr. Pinkem mentioned in his talk." He lightly rapped his knuckles against his forehead. "Oh, what were those called? A thylacine or something like that?"

"No, thylacines were called Tasmanian tigers or Tasmanian wolves," Micky said. "They probably went extinct about a hundred years ago."

"Oh, that's right."

"It was thyla-something." Izzy rubbed his chin.

"Uh, oh yeah, thylacosmilus."

Jax leaned his head back against the rest. "That's it." He turned to watch the animal. "It's really cool."

"I do wish we had time to learn more about all these animals." JT blew her bangs out of her eyes. "And wouldn't Dr. Pinkem be thrilled to know how accurate his research into the kinds has been? He'd love this."

Jax smirked. "Well, we have been studying them. We just tend to do it up close while running for our lives."

"That's true," Izzy said. "There's nothing quite like hands-on experiences."

Micky pulled herself forward using Izzy's seat and pointed toward the thylacosmilus. "Wait. Didn't Dr. Pinkem say that the fossils of those things are found in South America? What's it doing here?"

"All of the animals started around here after the Flood," Jax said. "They had to get off the Ark at the same place as everything else. So it isn't surprising to find them here in this time period. Maybe there just aren't any examples of them being fossilized in this region of the world."

"That's right," JT said. "It's like the kangaroos. Bethany tried using that argument on me before. She asked why we don't find kangaroo fossils in the Middle East if they really were on Noah's Ark." JT rolled her eyes and shook her head. "It's not as if every creature that dies gets fossilized. I explained to her that if they were killed by predators or even died naturally, then they wouldn't become fossilized. Only those buried rapidly under the right conditions can become fossils."

"Has anyone ever found evidence that kangaroos once lived outside of Australia?" Izzy asked.

"Not that I know of." JT shrugged.

"Actually, they have." Micky smiled and nodded enthusiastically. "Several years ago in western India, archaeologists found thousands of pictographs on rock walls and in caves depicting creatures, and some look a whole lot like kangaroos."

"Really?" JT asked. "I've never seen that."

"Dr. Chiler has some pictures of them here." Micky flipped through the book until she found the desired page. She spun it so everyone else could see. "Look."

The photographs showed cave paintings of animals, including five that looked like kangaroos or wallabies, complete with large pouched bellies. "That's cool," Jax said.

"Very." Izzy leaned in to get a closer look.

JT tilted her head as she studied the images. "That seems to fit the biblical worldview quite well. We know kangaroos must've lived somewhere between Ararat and Australia. What do evolutionists say about those paintings?"

"The archaeologist who found them hypothesized that they were drawn by people who had migrated from Australia to this part of India." Micky pointed to a caption beneath one of the photos. "But that view is questioned by many experts because of the vast distance and the difference in how kangaroos are depicted in Australian cave art. I suppose some people might argue that the paintings don't really represent kangaroos, but what else could they be?"

"Wow," JT said. "Okay, I'm sorry for teasing you about Dr. Chiler and her book. I'll have to check it out."

Micky gestured toward the creature near the stream. "So I guess the kangaroos would've been like this thylaco-whatever-you-called-it. They lived in an area but were never fossilized there."

"Or maybe some were but we haven't found them yet," Izzy said.

Micky gave a thumbs up. "Good point."

The thylacosmilus turned around and licked its paw before bounding back into the forest. As it disappeared from view, the sky darkened and a crack of thunder echoed around them. The rain grew heavier, pounding against the vehicle.

"Will the solar panels be safe out there?" JT asked.

Jax nodded. "They should be."

The storm lasted for nearly three hours. Izzy came close to finishing the mold before they played a variant of the alphabet game at JT's suggestion, in which each person named something they had witnessed during their trips to the past. JT started with *Ark*.

"I almost said 'Al,'" she said, laughing, "but I thought it might be too soon for poor Izzy. Plus, not even a real-live dinosaur could measure up to seeing the Ark."

Micky followed with *branch*, the cause of their latest brush with danger, and Izzy went with *carnotaur*, shooting JT a look that seemed to say he laughed in the face of rampaging carnivores. Although the game was a bit cheesy, Jax liked being reminded of their amazing and terrifying adventures. His description of the time machine's *xanthic* color was creative, but everyone else said it was a stretch. His favorite moment occurred when Micky cited *friends* and *faith* for the letter *F*. Of all the incredible things she had seen, the most amazing had been the other three people in the vehicle, who had risked their lives for her and led her to faith in Christ.

Jax enjoyed a catnap after the game, and JT woke him up once the rain let up and the sky brightened. Joined by Izzy, he filtered stream water to refill their water bottles and the bladder in JT's backpack. They hurried back to the car, and within a few minutes the vehicle hovered high above the trail through the forest.

Jax squinted as the sun dipped beneath the last of the gray clouds before them. A glance in the rearview mirror caused him to jerk his head around. "Whoa, check it out." A vibrant rainbow stretched over the trees not far behind them, its radiant colors striking a sharp contrast with the gray-black clouds behind it.

"Cool. I can see both ends," Micky said.

"How about a pot of gold?" Izzy asked.

Micky laughed. "Nope, I already checked."

JT glanced at Jax. "It's beautiful."

Jax gave her a half smile and nodded.

Izzy stretched his arms and sighed. "Hopefully, it's a sign that things are about to go better on this trip."

NINE

Almost finished. Izzy reversed the drill bit out of the hole and tapped it on a piece of plastic on the floor to shake off the grit. He picked up the mold and peered through the shaft he had just finished boring all the way through it. Satisfied that it was straight enough to make a wire, he plunged the drill back into one side and spun it several times to smooth the edges of the small tunnel. After turning the mold around, he repeated the process on the other side. Keeping one opening pointed toward the floor, he blew through the opposite end to clear out remaining debris.

He sighed and set the mold on the floor. "Done."

Jax flashed a sheepish grin. "Now we just need to find some silver and figure out how to melt it."

Izzy chuckled. "Is that all?" Traveling above the seemingly unending forest for the past thirty minutes had been relatively uneventful. "I wonder what time of year it is here."

"It feels like summer," Micky said.

Izzy shrugged. "Yeah, the weather does, but the days seem too short for that. It's just a guess, but I think it might be early spring. We're only getting about twelve to thirteen hours of daylight."

"I think you're right," JT said. "The sun was

never really too high in the sky today, and it was always a little toward the south."

Micky clicked her tongue. "You two should switch your majors to meteorology. Then maybe we could all go to the same school."

Izzy grinned and shook his head. "I'll pass."

As the girls chatted about potential majors, Izzy stared off toward the horizon. The sun continued to sink lower in the sky, and his mind wandered back to something Bethany had said. He waited for a lull in the conversation and then twisted around to face JT. "Hey, I've got another question. It's sort of like the one about the strange laws in the Bible."

JT raised her eyebrows. "Sure. Go ahead."

"Okay, so you know how the Bible talks about slavery, right?"

"Yep. In several places."

"So how come it never speaks against it?" Izzy tried to keep his voice steady.

JT furrowed her brow. "It does. The Bible describes the Israelites' slavery in Egypt in pretty negative terms."

"Sorry, that's not really what I meant." Izzy scratched his head. "Uh, I guess it'd be better to ask it this way: How come the Bible never outlaws it? You know, in the Old Testament there are rules for how you should treat a slave, but it doesn't just come out and say, 'set them free,' which seems like the best way to handle it. It makes it seem like God was okay with owning slaves."

"Don't you remember Pastor Rich talking about that at the last 'Stump the Pastor' night?" Micky asked.

Jax knitted his brow as he looked at Izzy. "I don't remember that. Do you?"

Izzy shook his head. "Nope." He turned to Micky. "Are you sure?"

"Yeah, he did." JT said as she tapped her phone's screen several times.

"Oh, that might've been the night you guys missed a couple months ago."

"Must've been," Izzy said. "Oh well, you two can fill us in."

"Hold on." JT scrolled through several blocks of text before she looked up. "Sorry, I was just trying to find a passage." She took a deep breath and let it out. "So, slavery and the Bible. Hm, where to start."

"Maybe where Pastor Rich did." Micky pulled one of her legs underneath her and sat up straighter. "He said that there were a few things to keep in mind when studying this issue. I think he started by talking about descriptive and prescriptive passages in the Bible."

JT pointed at her. "That's right. The Bible contains *prescriptive* passages, like the ones you alluded to where the Israelites were told how to treat their slaves. Then there are *descriptive* passages where we're just told what happened, and the Bible doesn't say that it was sanctioned by God." She pushed her bangs away from her eyes.

"Right," Micky said. "So *prescriptive* are ones that tell a person or group of people what to do. Like a doctor *prescribes* medicine with instructions to follow. And then *descriptive* are the narrative or historical passages that *describe* what happened."

"I think we already understood the difference," Jax said.

"Okay," JT said. "Well, skeptics will often read a descriptive passage and assume that the Bible approves of whatever it described, but that isn't necessarily the case."

"You mean like when Jacob pretended to be Esau to get his father's blessing?" Jax asked.

JT closed her eyes as if she were trying to remember every detail about that account. Finally, she looked at Jax. "Yeah, I think that's a good example. I don't think the Bible comes right out and tells us that what Jacob did was wrong, at least not there. I mean, it does tell us that lying is wrong, but this passage just describes what he did."

"Yeah, but that doesn't really cover the slavery issue," Izzy said. "After all, the Bible does have some prescriptive passages on the subject."

JT shrugged a shoulder. "It covers most of the passages about slavery, but yes, there are a few prescriptive ones." She looked at Micky. "Anything to add?"

Micky shook her head and then held up two fingers. "The second point is that most of the slavery mentioned in the Bible was quite different than what we usually think of when talking about slavery."

"Right. We typically think of what happened in the South, before the Civil War, when many slaves were severely beaten and treated almost like cattle or even worse." A frown formed on JT's face as she slowly shook her head. "But when God gave the law to Moses for the people of Israel, He included several rules about how slaves were to be treated. Oftentimes, it was more like indentured servitude. You know, if someone owed a debt or had committed a crime, they'd have to serve the person they owed or wronged for a set amount of time instead of going to prison. They weren't allowed to work on the Sabbath, so they had at least one day of rest every week. And after six years, if the person wanted to go free, then the owner was commanded to free them. So the prescriptive passages in Exodus and Leviticus set limits on slavery."

"That's right," Micky said. "It was part of their justice system. It wasn't about owning and mistreating a person because of how they looked."

Izzy bit his lip as he considered their words.

"Interesting. I'll need to think on that. What's the third point?"

JT exchanged a glance with Micky, who mumbled a few words to her. "You start," JT said.

"Okay, let's see if Izzy really is a genius." Micky giggled. "Did you know that one of the books in the Bible is written to a slaveowner?"

"A book written to a slaveowner." Izzy repeated the words as he tried to grasp their importance. "There is?"

"Yep." JT raised her eyebrows and smiled. "It's a short book in the New Testament, only one chapter long."

"Philemon?" Jax asked.

"Uh huh," JT said. "Philemon was a slave owner. His runaway slave Onesimus eventually became a believer, and he met the Apostle Paul. Paul sent him back to his owner in hopes that the men would be reconciled. The apostle urged Philemon to treat Onesimus as a brother rather than a slave."

Micky glanced at her friends. "I'm sure Bethany never brings up this point when she talks about the Bible and slavery."

Jax chuckled. "No, she'd never take the time to look closely at the issue. She just looks for things that will sound as bad as possible."

"That's for sure." Izzy's smile faded and he turned back to the girls. "Did Paul *command*

Philemon to free Onesimus?"

"Not exactly," JT said. "He definitely encouraged him to do it, but Paul was focused on sharing the gospel and planting churches. He wasn't seeking to overthrow the entire Roman civil system."

"What do you mean?" Izzy asked.

"That was kind of Pastor Rich's fourth point," JT said. "He mentioned that some historians have estimated that as much as one-fourth of the Roman Empire's population was made up of slaves. And remember, most of the slavery wasn't like in the United States prior to the Civil War. It wasn't based on a person's skin shade. Education was encouraged for slaves, and they were often better educated than their masters. They performed important social duties, and most of them were set free by the age of thirty."

"Yep," Micky nodded. "In a lot of cases, it was more like an employer and employee relationship."

JT pointed to her phone. "In Ephesians 6:5–9, Paul gave some instructions to both slaves and their masters. He essentially reminds them that we're all servants of God, and that God doesn't show favoritism to slave or owner. We'll all be held accountable for how we treat one another."

Izzy pursed his lips and stared past JT out the window at nothing in particular. "Okay, well that puts a whole different perspective on it. I guess when I hear the word *slavery*, it automatically makes me think of the past few centuries, and it's hard to imagine that God would support that."

"I'm sure He isn't okay with the idea of one human owning another," JT said. "That's not the way He designed this world, but sin has wrecked human relationships and has led to things like slavery."

Micky put a hand on the headrest behind Izzy. "And can you imagine what would've happened if Paul and others commanded everyone to free their slaves? The power of the whole Roman Empire would've been used to squash the early church, and they would've struggled to survive ... even more than they already did. Not to mention that a large portion of the population would've suddenly been jobless and homeless. But instead, the early Christians focused on planting churches, getting the gospel out, and caring for those in need. I think they believed that as men's hearts changed in response to the gospel, their attitudes toward institutions like slavery would change as well."

Izzy rubbed his neck as he considered their words. "That makes sense. It's sort of like the way Pastor Rich has talked about abortion. You can try to change the laws and fight for the rights of the unborn, but until people's hearts are transformed by the gospel, we won't see lasting change on that issue."

"Yeah," Micky said. "That's actually a pretty

good comparison."

"Whoa!" JT pointed toward the edge of the forest. "Slow down. I think I saw someone."

"What? Where?" As he scanned the area, Jax decreased their speed and lowered the car to a couple of feet above the trees. "Increase exterior mic, maximum volume."

Izzy leaned closer to the windshield. "I don't see anything. Was it the caravan?"

"I don't think so," JT said. "We'd probably be able to see some of their large animals if it were them."

The car crept forward as the trees became sparse. A raised area to their right ran ahead for approximately half a mile. Directly before them lay a vast open plain divided by what appeared to be a river far in the distance, but with the sun nearing the horizon, it was difficult to see in that direction.

"Right there," JT said as she pointed past Izzy.

"Yeah, I see them too." Jax slowed the car even more but allowed it to drift toward a large tree. "Even though we're cloaked, I think it's safer if we hide behind this for now."

While they inched forward, Izzy gazed at the scene unfolding before them. A man hauled a rock toward a wagon about half the size of a car. He grunted as he hoisted the stone into the bed and allowed it to drop with a thud. Covered in dirt, the man wore what appeared to be one long cloth wrapped around his waist and slung over his shoulder. He turned and walked back toward the hillside. As he disappeared from view, a similarly dressed man seemed to appear out of the hill.

"Where did he go?" Micky asked.

"It looks like they're going in and out of that hillside," Jax said. "And since they're carrying rocks—there's no way we already found a mine, is there?"

"It can't be that easy," Micky said. "But it sure looks like it."

JT yawned. "Well, we need to figure out if they're really mining here."

As the second man retreated into the hillside, Izzy focused on their dilemma. "And if so, what they're mining."

"Look there, past the wagon." Jax pointed a finger to the left of the cart. "It looks like some shelves carved into the side of the hill, and in each space there's some sort of metal object. I think they might be idols. I can't really tell from this far away."

"Interesting. It does look sort of like that." JT squinted as she studied the scene before them. "So how are we going to determine if this place has what we need?"

Izzy focused on the sunset before him. "I suggest we wait until these people leave for the night, assuming that they do. Then we sneak over there and check it out."

TEN

Izzy spun in his seat and faced JT. "Sorry, I've got another—"

"Alright, they've been gone for an hour. It should be safe," Micky said. "Sorry to interrupt you, Izzy."

"That's okay. I'll ask it later."

"Looks clear to me, too. What do you think?" Jax turned to JT and she nodded. "Okay, let's get down there." He raised the car a couple feet off the ground and piloted it toward the mine.

They had watched the laborers carefully for nearly half an hour and counted six in all. As night fell, the men ceased their work when two more individuals arrived with a pair of animals. The beasts were hitched to the wagon, and then the entire crew headed west along the base of the hill. Once they'd disappeared in the darkness, Jax had set the vehicle down to conserve power while they waited to be sure no one was returning.

"How close do you want me to park?" Jax asked as they neared the mine.

"I'd say at least fifty feet away, and you can keep it cloaked," Izzy said. "If someone returns, you don't want the car to be in the way or be easy to spot."

"Good point." Jax aimed for the opposite side

of the mine's entrance from the direction the people had gone. He slowed the car and lowered it to the grass. "How's this?"

"Works for me." Micky unbuckled her seatbelt.

"So did we decide who's going in with me?" Jax asked.

"I will." Micky tapped Izzy's shoulder. "That'll give you a chance to ask JT what you were about to bring up when I interrupted you."

"That works. But I want to get out of the car for a while," JT said. "We've been cooped up in here all day. Plus, I want to see those idols, or whatever they are, and see what they're made of."

"Yeah, that'd be the place to start," Izzy said.

Jax pulled out a small bag with his and Izzy's science fair project. "Here, take one of these so we can stay in touch when Micky and I head into the mine."

Izzy grabbed one of the earpieces. "Good idea."

After the girls each took one, the teens exited the vehicle. The mine's opening was tucked neatly into a small gap in the hillside. Using a flashlight to illuminate their path, Jax led the group past the entrance until they arrived at the rock wall. Five figurines rested within two-foot-tall alcoves.

JT pointed to the figure on the top right. "This one's made of wood. It kind of looks like an eagle."

"And this one is clearly stone." Jax shined the light on the one beneath it. "Not sure what it's supposed to be. Maybe a weird-looking human."

"Shine it over here." Izzy rested his hand on the wall next to the centermost idol.

Jax directed the light onto the statue, which looked like a man, but the form was rather rudimentary. The light reflected off the shiny surface. "That could be silver."

"That's what I was thinking," Izzy said.

"I wish we could just take it." Jax pointed at the object. "We could destroy an idol and get the silver we need to fix the machine."

"But that would interfere too much with the past," Izzy said.

Micky put a hand on her hip. "And it'd be stealing."

"Uh huh, that's why I said I *wish* we could do it." Jax glanced at each of them. "So are you okay with us taking silver from the mine? Is that stealing too?"

"If they haven't pulled it out of the ground yet, then they probably would never know that something was missing," Micky said.

"That's true," Izzy said. "But it could still impact that past."

"I know." Micky shoved her hands into her pockets. "But what other choice do we have? It'll change the past even more if we're stuck here for the rest of our lives."

Jax scanned their surroundings and then

nodded toward the entrance. "Should we check it out?"

"Definitely," Micky said.

They walked back to the mine and Jax pointed the flashlight into the tunnel. The opening was a little over five feet high and braced by wooden beams, much like the classic mine entrances seen in movies. A variety of tools rested just inside.

"How thoughtful. Looks like they left their tools for us to use," Micky said.

"Perfect." Jax spun and faced JT and Izzy. "You two should go back to the car. It'll be warmer. You can remain cloaked. And if you use the night vision and the exterior mic, you should be able to hear anyone or anything coming this way."

"Yeah, we will in a little while," JT said. "I'm not in a hurry to get back in there. Plus, I want to make sure we can still communicate with you once you're in there."

"Okay, but don't wait too long. It's better to be safe than sorry." Jax sighed. "Man, I'm starting to sound like JT."

She giggled. "Alright, you guys be careful."

"We'll let you know if we see or hear anything unusual," Izzy said.

"Make sure your earpieces are turned on and working," Jax said. "We'll let you know what we find while we're in there."

After each teen confirmed their devices were

properly working, Jax and Micky ducked under the lintel and entered the mine. Jax picked up something that looked like a pickaxe and Micky chose a crude hammer. As they took a few more steps, they were able to stand upright, but just barely. The temperature dropped about ten degrees and the scent of soil filled the air. Jax swept the flashlight back and forth as they moved down the tunnel. Every few steps brought them to another set of wooden supports on both walls and the ceiling. "Can you hear me?"

"Yes." JT's voice said through his earbud. "What do you see?"

"Nothing much so far," Micky said.

"Wait." Jax held up a hand and directed the light where the tunnel continued to the left. "Look there." Then he moved the light to the right and second path came into view. "We can go left or right."

"Which one seems to be used more?" Izzy asked.

Jax and Micky studied the floor. The trail to the left appeared to be wider, and the smoother floor showed that it witnessed more traffic.

Micky pointed and Jax nodded. "The left. We'll take that one first."

"Okay," Izzy said.

They moved slowly down the selected path and it looked the same as what they had seen so far.

Jax continually focused the light on the walls, searching for any hint of metal. "So how are your brother and sister doing?"

"Pretty good," Micky said. "I saw them a few weeks ago when I visited my dad's."

"You mentioned that you were looking for opportunities to witness to them. Anything come up?"

"Yeah, I had a couple of good conversations with Andrew. He's eleven now and asks a lot of questions. But Heather didn't really seem to understand much of what I said. She's only eight though, so I'm not surprised."

"That's awesome that you've been trying—"

JT's voice crackled in his ear. "Hey … breaking …"

Jax and Micky stopped and retraced their steps for a few seconds. "Can you hear me?"

"Yes, but not very well," JT said.

They moved a few more steps toward the opening of the mine. "How about now?"

"Yep, that's clearer."

"Alright, I guess this is where we say goodbye for a little while," Jax said. "We need to go farther in. You guys should go back to the car and stay alert. Remember, you must not be seen."

"I know," JT said. "Just be careful."

Jax smirked and glanced at Micky.

She rolled her eyes and chuckled. "Yes, Mother."

"We'll be fine," Jax said. "See ya soon."

As they walked, the soil scent gave way to more of a pungent sooty smell, and the air was cooler and stale. Before long, the tunnel banked around to the right and opened up into a classroom-sized space. "Cool," Jax said as he panned the light from one side of the room to the other. The walls lit up as the light hit them and the room grew brighter than he anticipated. "Looks like there's a good amount of quartz in here."

"That's a good sign. Remember, Izzy said that silver is often found with quartz."

Jax raised his eyebrows. "He did?"

Micky let out a mock sigh. "You need to do a better job of listening." She pointed ahead and to the right. "There. I think I saw something shiny."

Jax aimed the light and several specks glinted back at him. "Let's check it out."

They crossed the room and reached a rock wall containing quartz with hints of a gray or silvery metal in it. Micky turned to him. "This could be it."

Jax grinned. "Maybe our luck has finally changed after all."

"Luck?" Micky asked. "Maybe luck has nothing to do with it, and God just answered our prayers."

"Yeah, I agree," Jax said. "From a human perspective it seems like luck. Anyway, let's grab some of this."

"How do we separate the silver from the

quartz?" Micky asked.

"I assume we can break a lot of it with the hammer. Then if we're able to heat it up enough, whichever one has a lower melting point should flow out of it. And I think silver will melt before quartz."

For the next twenty minutes the teens chipped and hammered several baseball-sized rocks from the wall, each containing multiple chunks or streaks that might be silver. Micky placed each of them in a bag and then turned to Jax. "I think this is enough. We should probably get going."

They hurried back through the tunnel and when they reached the fork, Jax tried to connect with JT and Izzy. "Are you guys there?"

After a couple of seconds without a response, he looked at Micky. "They're probably in the car and not getting the signal." Still, a twinge of concern crept into his mind.

As they emerged from the mine, Jax took a deep breath of fresh air. "That's better."

Micky rubbed her arm. "And it's warmer out here. Come on, let's get out of here."

Jax increased his pace toward the vehicle. "Can you guys hear me?" When they still did not reply, his level of concern grew.

"Maybe the batteries are dead," Micky shrugged.

He shook his head. "Not likely. They should've

been fully charged." He shined the flashlight in the direction of the vehicle. "If the cloak is on, it might be hard to find." Jax stopped scanning when the light near the top of the beam struck a tree in the distance, but the light from the middle on down seemed to distort and dissipate about twenty feet in front of them. "There it is."

Jax hurried to the car, groped for the door handle, and pulled it. "Why didn't you guys—?" As he peeked inside, he realized it was empty. His heart raced and dread flooded into his mind. He glanced at Micky. "They're not here."

"Where could they be?" she asked. "Would they go for a walk?"

"No way. JT would say it was way too dangerous."

"That's true." Micky twisted her lips as she looked around. "Maybe they're just playing a prank on us. C'mon guys, it's not funny anymore."

The two stood silently until Jax realized that he was holding his breath. "I doubt that both sets of their earbuds stopped working." He glanced at the car. "We could honk the horn. That would get their attention and let them know we're back."

"Here let me see that," Micky said as she reached for the flashlight. Jax let her take it and she swept it across the meadow, focusing most of her attention on the side closest to the mine.

"I'm gonna hit the horn." Jax stepped back to

the car and ducked inside.

As he reached for the middle of the steering wheel, Micky held up a hand. "Wait!"

Jax ran around to the front of the vehicle. "What are you looking at?"

She led him back toward the mine. "I think I saw something shiny over here." Keeping the light aimed toward the ground, she pointed ahead. She scanned for three more seconds before stopping. "Right there."

"What is that?" Jax asked as they approached the object. A sickening feeling engulfed his body, and his stomach tied itself into a knot. "Izzy's glasses. Something's wrong."

Micky bent down and scooped them up. "Maybe they're hiding from something." She caught his eye. "Or someone."

"No. This can't be happening." His heartrate surged as his mind struggled to come to grips with the idea that tragedy may have befallen his friends. He stood and quickly looked in all directions. "JT! Izzy!"

Micky shushed him. "Not so loud. Let's get back to the car and search from there. We aren't going to do them any good if something happens to us."

They sprinted back to the time machine and climbed inside. Jax made sure the cloak and night vision were engaged before giving the horn a few short bursts. He gripped the steering wheel and fought unsuccessfully against the urge to panic. "We have to find them!"

Micky put a hand on his shoulder. "We don't even know what happened. Try to stay positive."

"I can't. If something happened to her—or to Iz." He bit his lip and turned to face the driver's side window as his eyes moistened.

"Jax, I need you to be calm so we can figure out how to find them. Remember, you're the optimist."

"But if they're—" An image of the T. rex catching JT and Izzy by surprise popped into his mind, and he shuddered. "No."

"If something happened, then we fix the time machine and go back to warn ourselves about this trip before it happens."

"But that would—"

"I don't care." Micky's face remained calm. "Whatever it takes." Somehow, the most impulsive member of their group kept her composure while he was falling apart.

Jax took a deep breath and stared straight ahead while trying to block out his overactive imagination. "Where do we start?"

Micky held his gaze. "With prayer."

Epilogue

Mr. Li withdrew his hand from the door, closed his eyes, and took a deep breath. *I don't want to do this.* Images of his family flashed through his mind: his wife and then Mei-Lin. *But what else can I do?* After opening his eyes, he rapped on the wood. The early afternoon sunshine beat down on him, giving him a convenient excuse for the sweat caused by his anxiety.

Several seconds later, the door opened, just a crack at first, and then Jax's father opened it wide and smiled warmly. "Ah, Mr. Li." He stretched out his hand and Mr. Li shook it. "What brings you over here on a Sunday?" His expression suddenly went blank. "Jax isn't in trouble, is he?"

Mr. Li chuckled and his nervousness waned a little. "No, he's not in trouble. Not at all." He took a deep breath. "In fact, I'd like to thank you and your wife for the privilege of teaching him for the past four years. He's been one of my favorite students."

"Oh, well thank you for saying that. I know you've been his favorite teacher." Dr. Thompson grinned, making it obvious to see where Jax's familiar smile came from. "Thanks for putting up with him."

"It was my pleasure. Is he here?"

"No, he's at our church camp until tomorrow night."

"Oh, that's right." Mr. Li shifted his weight as he tried to pretend that he had forgotten this information. He swallowed the lump in his throat, regretting the lie he was about to tell. "Listen, Jeff. Did Jax say anything about me stopping by to pick up a book I loaned him earlier this year?"

Dr. Thompson pursed his lips. "Not that I recall. Hold on." He turned away from the door. "Ellen, did Jax mention leaving a book for Mr. Li?"

"I don't think so," Mrs. Thompson's voice came from the living room somewhere beyond her husband.

He faced Mr. Li again. "She said—"

"I heard." Mr. Li's eyes grew wide. "Wait. He said he was going to leave it in the front seat of his car. Is that still here?"

"Yeah, give me just a sec." Dr. Thompson stepped behind the door and reappeared a moment later with a pair of sandals on his feet. "Be right back," he said to his wife. After stepping onto the short porch, he shut the door. "Let's go check."

Dr. Thompson led Mr. Li back toward the driveway and then turned right into the breezeway between the house and garage.

"Is this larger than the last time I saw it?" Mr. Li asked.

"You've been here before?"

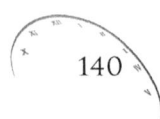

"Yes, two years ago." Mr. Li squinted as he thought back to that visit. "Almost exactly two years ago. It was the day after the science fair. I had to check out Jax's project since he and Izzy decided not to enter it in the fair. I guess that was shortly before you were rescued."

"That would've been a couple weeks before, yeah." After pressing his thumb to a scanner next to the door, Dr. Thompson punched in a lengthy code on the upper panel. A couple of beeps sounded from within the garage followed by a gentle click near the doorknob. Opening the door, he gestured for Mr. Li to enter. "To answer your question, this is more than twice as large as it was before."

When the lights came on, Mr. Li's jaw dropped slightly and he stared around the space. Lined with shelves full of lab equipment, the wall to their right reminded him of his classroom. An empty garage bay lay to his left, and Jax's car rested in the next stall, partially covered by a tarp. Workbenches loaded with tools and various projects filled up the near and far walls. "This is amazing. I'll bet you guys spend a lot of time out here. I know I would."

Dr. Thompson smiled. "Yeah, Jax and Izzy have practically lived out here the past two years. Sometimes I get a chance to join them, but I'm usually at my other lab—the one that pays me to be there."

"I understand." He spotted the toy car from the previous science fair on a nearby shelf. "Did you help out with their cloaking device?"

"Not really." Dr. Thompson stole a glance at the toy car. "I put them in touch with a friend from college who had done some pioneering work in that field, and I helped them manufacture the little rods. But I wanted them to do most of it on their own."

"That sounds like a good approach. It's wonderful that they have access to some great scientists."

Dr. Thompson nodded toward him. "You mean besides those at the school."

Mr. Li snorted. "Thank you. Yes, besides them." He wished he could enjoy a lengthy conversation in this space, but he had a more pressing task. *Don't forget why you came here.* He tilted his head toward Jax's car and tried to mask his frustration when he noticed its current state. "That sure looks different than last time. Are they overhauling it?"

Dr. Thompson shrugged. "I'm not sure. Those guys are always doing something."

"So did they really ever get that thing to work?"

The corners of Dr. Thompson's mouth turned up slightly. "What do you think?"

Mr. Li crossed his arms. "It's hard to imagine, but the kids told a compelling story." He caught Dr. Thompson's eye. "Did they ever take you on a trip?"

Dr. Thompson laughed. "You really do believe them, don't you?" He stepped toward the car and opened the passenger door. "What was Jax supposed to leave for you?"

"Oh, um, one of my physics textbooks that he borrowed. He said he'd put it in the car."

"Hold on."

As Dr. Thompson ducked into the vehicle, Mr. Li looked around the room again, but besides the car, nothing reminded him of a time machine.

Dr. Thompson backed away from the front seat. "It's quite a mess in here. Maybe it's in the back seat."

In the two seconds it took for Dr. Thompson to stand and move out of the way before closing the front door and opening the back door, schematics on the front seat grabbed Mr. Li's attention. The page contained multiple sketches of a sportscar with technical modifications, including hover devices like those on the bottom of Jax's car. The title on the top of one of the pages read "TM1" in large bold handwriting. *TM1?* Mr. Li spun and faced the toy car, fighting to contain his emotions. *Time Machine 1? But that's not Jax's car. Is there another one?*

Dr. Thompson stood up straight. "I'm sorry. I don't see any textbooks. He must've forgotten to leave it for you."

Mr. Li tried to give off a frustrated look

while rubbing the back of his neck. "Okay. Well, I suppose it'll just have to wait."

"Are you sure?" Dr. Thompson closed the car door. "I can go search his room if you really need it."

"No, that's okay. Maybe he can just bring it to graduation later this week." Mr. Li took a step toward the exit. "I'll send him a text to remind him. Thanks for checking."

"No problem at all." Dr. Thompson led him out the door and toward the driveway. "It was good to see you again, and thanks again for teaching Jax all these years."

"It really was a privilege. Sorry to interrupt your Sunday afternoon." Mr. Li waved as he started for his car. "Enjoy the rest of your weekend."

"Thanks. You too."

Mr. Li climbed into his car and slammed his head into the headrest. Shame filled him for lying to the father of one his students. *You had to do it. Lives are at stake.* As he buckled in and started the car, he thought again of his family and the wicked man who had threatened their lives. *What should I do? Can I even tell them about the other time machine and put Jax's family in danger?* He pulled out his phone and unlocked it. Staring at Mei-Lin's picture on the screen, he swallowed hard. He knew what he had to do.

THE AUTHOR

Tim Chaffey is a husband, father, cancer survivor, author, and apologist, with a passion for reaching young people with the gospel. He has earned a B.S. and M.A. in Biblical and Theological Studies, a Master of Divinity specializing in Apologetics and Theology, and a Th.M. in Church History and Theology.

Tim is the content manager for the Ark Encounter and Creation Museum. He is also the founder of Risen Ministries, which is home to his blog, podcast, and speaking ministry. He has written over two dozen books, including the following nonfiction titles:

In Defense of Easter: Answering Critical Challenges to the Resurrection of Jesus.

God and Cancer: Finding Hope in the Midst of Life's Trials

Fallen: The Sons of God and the Nephilim

Fans of the Truth Chronicles may also enjoy *The Remnant Trilogy*. This historical fiction series follows Noah from young adulthood up until the Flood. Tim coauthored these books for high school age and adults, and they serve as the official backstory for Noah and his family at the Ark Encounter.

THANKS

I would like to thank the people who helped make this series a reality.

My wife deserves much of the credit—Casey is my primary brainstorming partner and initial editor. Many of my favorite scenes were greatly enhanced by your involvement.

Thank you to Joe, Kayla, Sierra, and Rachel for your creative input and feedback in the final three books.

A very special thank you goes to editor Reagen Reed. I have learned so much about writing fiction from you, and this series is far better because of you. I'm very grateful for your contributions.

Another very special thank you to Melissa Mathis (a.k.a. Inkhana) for her incredible artwork. Thank you for using your talents for our Lord and Savior Jesus Christ and for your efforts to glorify Him through the use of Manga. I cannot imagine *The Truth Chronicles* without your illustrations. Thank you!

Finally, I want to thank my Lord Jesus Christ for saving me from my sin, giving me eternal life, and providing me with the opportunity to write these stories. I pray they will continue to encourage young believers and perhaps introduce others to our Creator and Savior.

If you have enjoyed these books, would you kindly consider leaving a positive rating and review at Amazon or Goodreads? This is one of the best ways to help an author promote his or her work.

"Like" The Truth Chronicles on Facebook for news, additional pictures, trivia, and more: www.facebook.com/thetruthchronicles

Made in the USA
Middletown, DE
15 September 2021